EUROSCHLOCK NIGHTMARES

Also from Muzzleland Press

Behold the Undead of Dracula: Lurid Tales of Cinematic Gothic Horror

Terror in 16-bits

EUROSCHLOCK NIGHTMARES

LURID TALES OF CINEMATIC CONTINENTAL HORROR

Edited by Jonathan Raab

MUZZLELAND PRESS

Muzzleland Press
Victor, NY

CATALOGO

"Being that they're made for the American film market, one must shoot them with that slightly childish mindset. I don't mean to badmouth the Americans—I have much respect for them—but they have a childish mentality. They want films of that kind. They want such 'terror' films, set in the castle. Maybe because they're made for children, I don't know. They want this kind of film. If you make a smart proposal, it's unlikely they're going to accept."

- Mario Bava

DIABOLICAL! FIENDISH! SAVAGE! AN INTRODUCTION TO THE SENSUALITY AND SURREALITY OF EUROSCHLOCK

Brian O'Connell

In her benighted bedchamber, the countess stalks to the window: wide-eyed, shroud-white, plagued by nameless terrors. Through the fluttering lace curtains, she glimpses the desolate family crypt, luminous in an unearthly gloaming, and, high above her, the indifferent moon, peering coldly through a tumult of black clouds as if to return her clandestine gaze. Time slackens till it melts. She's in the bed again, long strands of her lustrous dark hair strewn across the linen pillow, black brushstrokes on a blue canvas. A single slash of lavender light illumines her anxious eyes peering back and forth. The shadowy chamber is slowly surveyed: the lattice lurid with moonlight, vague impressions of inhospitably ornate furniture, ghostly tongues of flame licking the last logs in the fireplace. And from afar—growing louder—the heavy tread of mud-caked boots. She rises from the bed, sighs of dread rising steadily, staring fixedly at the door.

The silver noose-shaped handle is creaking...*turning*...twisting in its achingly slow axis. She can't scream—can barely breathe—and pins herself to the wall in a posture of decorous desperation. Slowly, the door groans open. The boots, clotted with grave-filth, cross the streams of moonlight. With an agonized gasp, she spies her intruder standing before the window: his looming silhouette framed by the heavy drapings, a riding crop weighed ominously in one hand.

"Kurt—*Kurt!*" she cries. The name of her tyrannous lover, dead and buried, suddenly offering itself as an awful, inevitable solution. She buries her head in her palms as if attempting to abolish him, but when she looks back up, an even worse sight is unveiled. His hand, corpse-green, clutched in a rigid claw so that it resembles some monstrous spider, pushes unwaveringly toward her, relentless, inexorable. Half-swooning, she rolls onto her back, affecting terror or submission or both. When the phantom hand finally alights on her head, her cries of fright dissolve almost imperceptibly into anxious moans of pleasure. She writhes beneath his cruel caress. He strokes her back lovingly before alighting on the ream of her nightgown. He pauses. Then, in one violent gesture, he tears the back of her dress open, exposing the vulnerable naked flesh. As he does so, disappearing into the night with this perverse act of sadistic affection, she lets out a single hoarse, inarticulate *grunt*: at once Poe's "groan of mortal terror" and the animalistic yelp of lust.

This ravishing sequence—with its sensuous mingling of eros and thanatos, sleaze and style, prurience and pure terror—came into being, as it only ever could have, under the immaculate direction of Mario Bava. The year was 1963, the actors Daliah Lavi and Christopher Lee, the film a sadomasochistic shocker entitled *The Whip and the Body* (alternatively known, under its perplexing US retitle, as *What!*). Today considered an early triumph, *The Whip and the Body* offers a striking synthesis of the formidable generic mastery on display in the filmmaker's venerable string of B-horror masterstrokes, which deftly traverse the antiquarian trappings of the Gothic (*Black Sunday,*

Kill, Baby...Kill!) and the grislier terrain of the giallo and the slasher (*Blood and Black Lace, A Bay of Blood*) alike. The influence of Bava's consummate artistry upon the horror genre as a whole has been likened to Hitchcock's. Bava's son, Lamberto, eventually picked up the family tradition, directing genre movies well into the late nineties. His first film, a gruesome nightmare of cannibalism and dismemberment dubbed, simply and fittingly, *Macabre*, was screened for his father just two months before his death: an occasion upon which the elder Bava is said to have remarked, with ironic satisfaction, "Now I can die at peace."

Taken together, the careers of this father-son duo span the length of an era in European horror cinema rightly characterized as a golden age, albeit one whose exact parameters continue to be debated. This much is clear: throughout the latter half of the twentieth century, the nations of continental Europe—most famously Italy, France, and Spain—produced a glut of cheapie horror flicks the likes of which the (under)world had never seen before. They flooded the largely rural, third-rate movie houses of their home nations; abroad, they loomed large and ghastly in the gutter grindhouse joints of 42nd Street or on the grand faded screens of countryside drive-ins. That is, provided they were permitted to be screened at all, and not banned or censored under the ignominious label of violent pornography (as many were, infamously, in the United Kingdom's "video nasty" persecution during the early eighties). One can understand why the uptight were so spooked: most of these movies projected a powerfully abject mix of violence and eroticism, pushing the on-screen ratio of blood and bare skin to astounding new heights. The gnarliness of the gore and the seediness of the sex consigned them to the same reviled—yet immensely profitable—cultural space as the exploitation genre, with which they often overlapped.

But their appeal isn't reducible to the mere

scopophilic delights of guts and groins. The finest films of this era are also flat-out *weird*, their sheer strangeness just as alluring as their sleaze. Limited budgets and often nakedly exploitative intentions nonetheless often yielded aesthetically potent, sometimes even genuinely *artful* results, producing horror movies capable of occupying multiple points in the wild, rangy spectrum between the arthouse and the grindhouse. This is a singular cinema that is often just as enamored with the pleasure of design as it is with the spectacle of knives sinking into skin; that destabilizes narrative even as it delivers on grisly thrills and knuckle-white suspense; that utterly collapses the false binary between the obscene, the shocking, and the outright *bad* on the one hand, and the beautiful, the intelligent, and the exquisitely elegant on the other. Call it Euroschlock.

That snappy label admittedly covers such a varied body of work that it's difficult to define too specifically. It's a word that embraces an incredibly wide range of national and regional contexts, and indeed specific auteurs, which don't always have much to do with one another. The ecstatically stylized abstractions of Dario Argento, the squalid grue and grotesquerie of Lucio Fulci, the decadent quasi-Symbolist poetics of Jean Rollin—all of these filmmakers are recognizably "Euroschlock," but are vastly divergent as stylists and thinkers. Anyone hoping to outline what made this moment in horror history unique has to be wary of flattening those many diversities, and no outline should ever be taken as definitive. Euroschlock is a beast that resists taxonomization.

A more materialist analysis of the movement might begin with an examination of the concrete production circumstances of these films, an arena in which some generalizations can be reasonably made. With a few lavish exceptions, Euroschlock is an almost invariably low-budget subgenre. Producers, then as now, were attracted to horror's simultaneous capacity for cheap production values and lucrative profits. Shooting schedules tended to be fairly tight. Scripts were fast-tracked; runtimes were concise. Within certain studio contexts—Italy most notably—repurposed sets and even recycled footage, lightly disguised, are visible across different films. The infamous prevalence of post-dubbed speech, a defining feature not only of Euroschlock but of commercial European cinema during this period in general, was not only necessitated by these films' international aspirations (one thinks of Douglas Sirk's famous aphorism: "The film has to fly in Kansas City and in Singapore!"), but also merely by the steep costs of synchronized sound tech: often an unaffordable expense for these scrappy productions. Even in its native language, the speech in Euroschlock is inevitably (and quite noticeably) imposed upon the image in post, a rather awkward and sometimes ghastly effect that nonetheless adds to the dreamlike artifice which lends these films their peculiar charm.

The bottom line underscoring these restrictive production circumstances demanded sensationalism first and foremost. Euroschlock was pitched to crowds very different from the mostly bourgeois attendees of the arthouse or the middle class patrons of popular first-run theaters. Both in its home nations and abroad, Euroschlock was distributed primarily to working class and even underclass settings—third-run moviehouses and drive-ins, usually—before potentially reaching eventual television syndication, typically in butchered format. The terms of audience engagement in those theatrical settings were radically different than those of the mainstream moviegoing public—more akin to the distracted and equivocal attentiveness of the television viewer than the reverent, concentrated involvement extolled by cinephiles.

The goal was not primarily to seduce the audience through narrative, but simply to keep eyes on the screen, a task at which pure shock tactics succeeded most amply and efficiently. Gruesome spectacles of stunningly excessive gore played a central role, of course, but if Euroschlock filmmakers hoped to compete with the newfound commercial dominance of pornography and "skin flicks," they had to employ an equal amount of freaky sex—the stranger, the better. The result, in a sterling confluence of Linda Williams' paradigmatic "body genres," was a cinema that aimed to operate directly upon the viewer's *corpus*: not so much a cohesive viewing experience as a calculated sequence of intense physiological *moments*, like the dizzying dips of a roller coaster or the involuntary jolts from an electrode.

Of course, many a lurid ad campaign promised sensations that the films themselves failed to deliver. But even when the visual transgressions weren't up to snuff, Euroschlock's structural innovations pierced much deeper. One might make the case that the subjugation of conventionally structured narrative to style and effect is, in fact, Euroschlock's defining contribution to the horror film genre. This is not to say that such films hadn't existed before the 1960s (Carl Theodor Dreyer's 1932 *Vampyr*, a haunting ramble through pure Gothic abstraction, is probably the most important precedent), but Euroschlock recoups that strategy from isolated experiments and makes it the foundation of an entire subgenre.

Its singularity is especially marked when we compare Euroschlock with the contemporaneous horror cinema of England and America. The classic genre pics put out by Universal in the thirties and forties, as well as their bloodier reincarnation in the Hammer productions of the fifties, sixties, and seventies were largely beholden to a classically Hollywood mode of narrative and aesthetic unity. These foundational films are linear, precise, and harmonious in their effects; they are beholden to a conservatism of narrative structure and theme alike, favoring relatively logical progression in the first department and the triumph of good over evil in the second. (Some of the B-horror movies of producer Val Lewton, which anticipate Euroschlock in their menacing irresolution and heightened aesthetics, are exceptions to this trend.) But the horrors of the Second World War had increasingly sapped these fusty fiends of their potency, to the point that they were reduced to mere objects of pop culture prankery, props for comedians like Abbott and Costello. Even Terence Fisher's grislier reanimations of the Universal movies remain heavily rooted in a premodern, anti-Enlightenment Christian rhetoric, whereby the humanity of the heroes, aided by the forces of God, ultimately overcome the disastrous perversions wrought by the scientific and the Satanic.

Euroschlock retains a vestigial, quasi-parasitic connection to Hollywood cinema. Most Euroschlock films were produced quickly to follow short-term commercial trends, and the accelerated production conditions of most of the films often made imitation a practical necessity. Echoes of the Universal monster movie, the Hammer Gothic, and, later on, subgenres like the Romero zombie are thus apparent across many European horror movies of this period. But these citations have been refracted through decades of historically European artistic reference points: perhaps most importantly, the Decadent movement of the nineteenth century and the Surrealist movement of the early twentieth, artistic philosophies that prized the totally subjective, the confoundingly irrational, and the aesthetically overripe.

Where classic Anglo-American horror is streamlined, coherent, and specific in its effects, Euroschlock favors the baroque, the outright outlandish. The "plots" of Euroschlock, such as they are, tend to be byzantine, not infrequently nonsensical, rife with loose threads and uncanny intrusions. They proceed by a sort of associative dream-logic, within which points of viewer identification are amorphous and interchangeable, the movement of narrative by no means progressive or even causal, and the construction of "reality" entirely subordinated beneath the genre's compulsive obsession with dread and death. More often than not, the lure that holds the viewer's attention is found in the image itself, whether in the form of sheer ghastly spectacle—and Euroschlock does amply deliver on tableaux of dismemberment, blood-letting, decomposition, and torture in their vilest forms—or, in the case of its finer auteurs, the pictorial pleasures of color and composition. Argento's *Suspiria* (1977) justly remains the most iconic example of this synthesis, its spare fairy tale narrative of occult conspiracy and demonic predation refracted through an astoundingly hallucinatory Technicolor visual kaleidoscope, like Disney colliding with Aubrey Beardsley. Euroschlock perhaps found no more self-representative image than that of *Suspiria*'s first victim: a young girl's corpse frozen in a simultaneously ecstatic and cataclysmic scream, her head haloed by a shatter of stunning stained glass.

In many respects, Euroschlock's skew toward abstraction in narrative and style meant that it wound up having more in common with the thriving international art cinema than with its more obvious forebears in Anglo-American genre pictures. Only a year after the 1960 release of Bava's breakout *Black Sunday*, *Last Year at Marienbad* would frustrate standard sense-making procedures with its cryptic, oneiric structure—qualities which most Euroschlock, even in its crummier instances, shares in spades. This relationship was by no means one-sided. Such recognized arthouse classics as *Eyes Without a Face* (Franju, 1960), *The Damned* (Visconti, 1969), *Salò, or the 120 Days of Sodom* (Pasolini, 1975), and *In a Glass Cage* (Villaronga, 1986) have much in common with the genre "trash" that academia so often unduly sets them against.

Like those art films, Euroschlock was responding to its time. Europe in the twentieth century, it hardly needs saying, was subjected to its fair share of seismic social ruptures, horrific revelations, and tragic repressions. Horror cinema, from its earliest inception in the silent era, was always addressing social reality (if only to deny it), but the horrors of the postwar period—the mass atrocities perpetrated by fascist regimes, the profound violence of colonialism, the apocalyptic shadow of nuclear weaponry, the creep of Friedmanite economics, the shockwaves of terrorism, the Iron Curtain's hard division of the entire continent by two antagonistic neo-imperial powers—demanded a more radical form than any that had been attempted before. It was no longer viable, as in *The Cabinet of Doctor Caligari* (1920), to relegate horror to a single individual's subconscious. Now reality *itself* was indisputably distorted, malevolent, and oppressive. The fractured form of Euroschlock, where logic sags beneath the weight of the grotesque, was ideally suited to reflect that traumatic new epistemology.

In his book *Euro Horror: Classic European Horror Cinema in Contemporary American Culture*, to which this introduction is heavily indebted, Ian Olney makes a case for Euroschlock as the prime harbinger in the horror genre of that much bandied-about term: postmodernity. Euroschlock's penchant for pastiche and hybridized influences already reflect a form of "postmodern" aesthetic innovation; so, too, does its assertion of absolute subjectivity, its disinterest in narrative, and its exalting of pure style. But these playful novelties cease to be mere shock games when they come into contact with history and politics, and, in Euroschlock's finer examples, they often do. Argento's films, for example, are heavily haunted by the repressed atrocities of the Holocaust: the phantom eagle in *Suspiria* that induces the savage murder of a blind man on the Munich *Königsplatz*; the rather fancifully-named "Richard Wagner School for Girls" in *Phenomena* (1985), in which pedagogy and classical European culture are linked to the filthiest forms of violence. The abomination of colonialism and its horrific reincarnation in Vietnam rears its head in many a zombie/ cannibal chiller, perhaps never more provocatively or disquietingly than in Ruggero Deodato's infamous *Cannibal Holocaust* (1980), where even the apparatus of filmmaking is revealed to be a corrupt and compromised exertion of power: self-reflexive, self-critical exploitation. Gialli generally interrogate lineages of gendered violence, the specific identity of the ubiquitous black-gloved killer far less important than the inescapable grip of his murderous hands and the many mangled female bodies he leaves in his wake. Fulci's movies often depict an indiscriminately and incoherently terrorizing universe where institutions of supposed rationality are themselves but mere permutations of evil. *The House by the Cemetery* (Fulci, 1981) even features a villain named Doctor Freudstein, the foundational modern philosophy of psychoanalysis satirically personified as a murderous monster. But if Fulci's critique echoes that of the Hammer Frankenstein films, his is nonetheless a crueler cosmos, lacking in any of Terence Fisher's pre-modern Christian comforts. *The Beyond* (1981), one of Fulci's most profoundly disturbing achievements, ends on a desolating vision of a fog-shrouded super-terrestrial wasteland from which there is no glimmer of escape or redemption. The ashen, corpse-strewn vista visually evokes the bomb-blasted landscapes of the two great wars, or the nuclear annihilation wrought at Hiroshima and Nagasaki. It's nothing less than the nightmare topography of the twentieth century itself.

These brief observations about specific films are not meant to ascribe a coherent or consistent ideological program to the whole of Euroschlock—far from it! Euroschlock's virtue lies precisely in its *refusal* of a single stable viewing point, of the aesthetic and thematic cohesion that might allow us to neatly fix some intrinsic essence underpinning its grisly spectacles. The uncanny dubbing, the wildly amalgamated influences, the spacey non-narratives, the visual overstimulation, the endless onslaught of gore and moribund eroticism: these jarring elements, so disharmonious when measured by the standards of mainstream cinema, collectively form an experimental aesthetic that legitimately reflects the pervasive terror and confusion that defines postmodern life. Moreover, these devices liberate the spectator from the strictures of specificity, opening endless avenues for interpretation in ways that still feel radical and rare for the genre. *This* is the source of Euroschlock's most potent power, its revolutionary value, when compared to the often over-prescribed meanings of contemporary horror cinema, its freshness and vitality is all the more apparent.

Of course, the PoMo potential in Euroschlock—its dislocated diegeses, murderous mise-en-abymes, anarchic absurdity—renders it uniquely compelling in our own era of political terror and ontological crisis. But, in addition to all these scholasticisms, let's not neglect the plain old fun factor. Euroschlock's surrealistic, shaggy surfaces provide an exhilaratingly wide range of opportunities for viewer pleasure, from conventional cinematic engagement to ironized distanciation to purely technical appreciation of effects and craft to the simple, satisfying squelch of a fake knife sliding into fake flesh. Horror and humor, spectacle and sadism, mystery and pure bafflement—all on offer for the spectator. In contradiction to the ever-narrowing horizons of Hollywood cinema, the choices here are endless. Such are the singular joys of this vibrant creative period in exploitation-entertainment, to which the writers of the stories you are about to read have attempted to pay fitting homage.

May they prove worthy offerings to all of us for whom—much like Bava's haunted countess, swooning in thanatotic rapture beneath Christopher Lee's phantom hand—the cold grip of fear is also the profoundest pleasure.

INCIDENT AT PUZZLE POINT

Patrick Lacey

So," Jack Cross says, "what the hell do you want?"

His face is a desert of wrinkles and silver stubble. Smoker's lines would be an understatement for the fissures that guard his mouth like fleshy parentheses. He lights a hand-rolled cigarette, breathes deep, fills the cramped, sterile room with sweet tobacco fumes.

For a sliver of a moment, the smoke eclipses him. That's not Jack behind the haze, but something that's never known the sun and never will.

"I'm Sherri?" I say. "Sherri Watson. We spoke on the phone about the interview. I won't take up much of your time. I know you're a busy man."

"I've heard that before. 'Won't take more than a few minutes, Mr. Cross.' But a few minutes is always more like an hour I won't get back." His Italian accent is distant, having moved to Hollywood in the late seventies. Still, it comes out to play every fifty words or so, probably more when he's drunk.

"We won't need an hour," I say.

Not for what I've got planned, I don't say.

He takes another drag on his handcrafted cigarette and sips coffee from a chipped mug. The logo's faded but in the right light, the Rorschach forms a castle where two actresses died on screen and off.

Or maybe I'm just seeing things.

"Let's start with how you came to be involved with *The Horror at Puzzle Point*."

He snickers at the mention of his most infamous film in a catalogue of infamous films, but his eyes go wide for a nanosecond. Even cynics get spooked.

"You're about eight years too late."

"Believe me, Mr. Cross, it's not my intention to dig up...difficult subjects. I know the families blamed you."

"Don't forget the public."

"And the public. But I'm not a journalist and I'm not here to point fingers."

"What are you then?"

I mentioned that on the phone too, but I let it slide. Jack Cross's patience lasts as long as one of his cigarettes, which is to say, it burns quick. "I write for a magazine. A *horror* magazine. It's called *More Gore*. 'For fans by fans.' That's our motto. My column is about re-evaluating modern classics."

"'Classic,' huh? That's one way to put it."

"I'm being sincere. It's a favorite of mine."

"You know what? I bet it is. But can we cut the bullshit?"

"What bullshit would that be?"

Jack takes another long drag, sips his coffee before the smoke can escape his lungs. I'm not sure how he does it. Then again, the man is a puzzle himself, one I'd like to put together, then disassemble just as fast.

"You're not here because of the movie. You're here for blood."

Jack's office isn't how you'd imagine. There's no floor-to-ceiling shelves housing film history tomes or canisters of precious 35mm prints. There's no shelves at all. The walls are bare save for a photo of what might be his fourth or fifth wedding and a framed, yellowed news clipping calling him a godless hack.

The reason I'm here today is exactly what I told Cross. I'm writing a piece for *More Gore*, one I had to push hard for. Bryce Clifton, my editor, thinks it's controversy for controversy's sake. He's not wrong. What sold him was my personal angle in all this. But like any self-respecting writer, I'll bury that lede. For now.

The Horror at Puzzle Point is a 1980 Italian horror film about a group of contest winners chosen to spend one night in a medieval castle filled with hidden treasure. The catch: it's also filled with secret passageways, booby traps, and a host of bloodthirsty foes, both human and inhuman. If it sounds unoriginal, that's because it is. But the plot is not the point. Like most European horror of the time, narrative is secondary to atmosphere and a sense of the surreal. The film is scary precisely *because* it makes no sense. At least that's my theory. Others would disagree.

Point was a critical failure but it still tripled its meager budget once word of the real-life deaths got out. It's true the events happened after production but they occurred on site at the film's main location, Holden Castle, where several of the cast members threw an unsanctioned wrap party. They planned to remain in the front wing, but you know how it goes. Curiosity killed more than just the cat.

"I was a hired gun," Jack says. "I did it as a favor to Claudio. And in return, he promised to make some calls. There was a script of mine dying a slow death on some producer's desk. He said he could move that script further up the pile."

"Did you believe him?" I say.

"Not for one minute. But Claudio was a friend and a mentor, not to mention my hero. What was I going to say?"

That would be Claudio LoGrasso, one of Italy's most vibrant genre filmmakers. He cut his teeth on westerns, giallo, and Gothic rip-offs of Hammer films. Like Cross, he was heralded as either a genius or a hack. He wrote the screenplay for *Puzzle Point* and was poised to direct but suddenly became ill during pre-production.

"I was between films," Cross says, "which is a nice way of saying 'out of a fucking job.' I was set to shoot an action picture but it went south days before we started shooting. That taught me a valuable lesson: a movie's not set in stone until you see it on the screen for yourself."

I smile, nod for him to go on. He doesn't. The thing about Cross is he hates interviews. It's a miracle I'm here today. You've got to coax him into answering or you're out of luck. Good thing I can be persuasive.

"To back up a bit, I'd like to discuss Mr. LoGrasso's illness."

Cross rolls his eyes until it's just the whites. It's straight out of *Puzzle Point*, in particular the scene where Wendy falls through a trap door into a subterranean chamber. The walls are made of pitted stone and a chandelier fashioned from bone offers meager light. Once she recovers, she finds herself staring at a roughly seven-foot-tall statue, one just out of focus for the audience. Whatever she sees, it terrifies her to the point of blindness. Her eyes take on the milky sheen of cataracts and she's left to stumble through the chamber until a man sporting an executioner's hood finishes what the statue started.

Said statue was a prop. The chamber was not. The crew stumbled upon a hole in the castle's basement, then begged the owner, one James Holden III, to use it. He said, "Do whatever you want. Just leave me alone." Producers asked if he'd known about the sub-basement. His response? "Of course not. This castle's always changing."

"Claudio was out of gas," Cross says. "Nothing more to it. Guy worked himself stupid for two decades without a break. Anyone would've gotten sick after a while."

"But it wasn't just exhaustion. He suffered a break with reality and spent three months at a psychiatric facility. The staff there claimed he was talking about the film as if it were real."

"That's what the press said, sure. But I knew Claudio. He flew to Hawaii and drank himself into a coma for a few months. Big deal."

Cross's eyelids flicker wide before evening out again. He sips more coffee to create a distraction since he doesn't believe half of what he's saying.

Claudio's mental health troubles are well documented. On the night of his admission to the facility, his neighbors phoned police when they heard him screaming. When officials arrived, they found the man on his balcony, naked as his premiere on Earth. His hands were held high to the sky. He shouted "Don't you see it? Can't you *feel* it?"

The event mirrors a scene in the script he'd penned just months before. Boris, the group's tour guide, hails a winged creature near the film's climax, after most of the cast has been killed off in inventive and odd ways. The flapping thing latches onto Boris' shoulder, flies him toward a moon the color of Merlot. His screams echo throughout the night, though it's unclear if they're from pain or ecstasy. As for what the creature is, we're never given an explanation, much like the rest of the film.

"Let's take five," Cross says, laying on the sarcasm thick as spackle. "If you don't mind."

He stands and leaves me alone in his office. This is the part where I'd snoop if there were anything worthy of snooping. Cross's desk has no drawers. It's a slab of wood with four legs and a rotary phone. There are no hiding places in this drab room. It's nothing like Holden Castle, known for its disguised passageways. There's a reason it was chosen for *Puzzle's* location. James Holden III inherited some fortune or another, one he used to assemble a castle in the fishing village of Gloucester, Massachusetts. I say "assemble" because his home is Frankensteined together, its architecture incorporating various authentic medieval dwellings shipped over from the continent. Inside, you're liable to start in a parlor from Brussels then wander into an Irish chamber. He lives the life of a recluse, has scarcely been seen in public since he was a child. He hires help to run errands, shop—anything that requires leaving the premises. Even during filming, the cast never once saw him. The man is obsessed with secret switches and other such contraptions. There's a hidden room deep within the castle's innards that can only be accessed via a series of levers and knobs, turned just so. One could even say *Puzzle Point* was written with Holden Castle in mind, even if Claudio denied knowing of its existence when he penned the script.

I stand and stretch, my lower back aching from yesterday's double and the double before it. *More Gore* pays enough to cover most of my electric bill. Bartending's much more lucrative. It's long hours and there's more creeps than Cross has cigarettes but the pay's decent. Just for a few months. That's what I told myself when I quit teaching to go freelance. A few months was three years ago. In that time, there were two boyfriends, both of which ended badly. Each accused me of preferring fiction to reality, that I was more comfortable with film than living my own life. It's like they were sharing notes. Also, they're right.

There was family, too, but we'll get to that.

I read through the news clipping. In a real-life plot twist, it's a review of the film I've come to discuss.

"A PUZZLE NOT WORTH SOLVING" reads the headline.

Director Jack Cross (*The Band Camp Murders*) offers up a film devoid of plot or sense. Events happen with no regard for structure. Characters are introduced and not seen or heard from again for half the runtime.

The set-up is trite, to put it generously. Five strangers are given the chance to search for treasure in a haunted castle riddled with traps and villains. From there, the film lacks any sort of cohesion. One character loses her sight from a statue. Another reaches into what she thinks is a chest of gold, only to find a wriggling mass of maggots that engulf her whole. Perhaps the most baffling scene involves a room-turned-chapel where robed cultists whisper to each other for several minutes straight. The words are never revealed and the figures are never mentioned again.

One has to imagine the film would've died a much slower death if it weren't for the real deaths of cast members Anna Larson and Kimberly Fontana following production. Those looking for grizzly murders and violent depictions of rape may enjoy this film. For all others, sit this one out.

"It's not exactly a Hollywood star," Cross says.

I hadn't heard him come in. I wonder how long he's been standing there.

"Plenty of films aren't appreciated in their time," I say. "I could name a dozen right now."

"I bet you could. Problem is, this one *still* isn't appreciated. I don't think your little article's going to change that." He's refilled his mug with black coffee. An oily sheen floats atop the surface like gasoline. In the right light, it's hypnotizing. It reminds me of another kind of darkness, the kind that brought me here today.

"Ready for some more questions?" I say, not really asking.

"It's getting late," he says. "I'd appreciate if we hurried this up. Smoke?" He slides one from his breast pocket.

"Never touch the stuff. My father died of lung cancer."

"Should've rolled his own." He flicks open a lighter, gets the tip going, shoves it into his lips. "Where were we?"

I ask him boilerplate questions about the film's production, about what he thinks the strange scenes mean.

"Why do you suppose so many things are left unexplained? Horror has a tendency to show its audience too much, to pull back the curtain too far, but some have said the film is too vague for its own good. It's true that much of European horror is light on logic but yours puts them all to shame. If there's any logic to be found, it's the nightmare kind."

"You're starting to sound like a critic. I don't like critics."

"I'm asking for your interpretation."

"I don't interpret my films, least of all one written by Claudio."

Bartending has taught me to keep a neutral face, no matter how vile the customer. Your old fashioned isn't strong enough? Let me fix that for you. Took me too long to get your order? This one's on the house. You make better tips that way. But Cross is testing my patience. He may be a private person. He may also be a hardened cynic. But he doesn't know I've brought more than questions with me.

"Let's talk about the Sobbing Woman," I say.

This time, he doesn't bother hiding his shock.
I take great joy in that.

Like any great urban legend, the Sobbing Woman's origins are murky at best. She appears in the background of several scenes: a woman standing a little over five feet tall, wearing an off-white dress and a veil that covers ashen skin. Her eyes glow green, allowing the viewer the slightest glimpse at her face. Her teeth are long and jagged. They sprout from her lips like blades of grass in need of trimming.

When she's on screen, the sound of crying can be heard on the audio track. You could make the argument she's like anything else in the film—an apparition placed there for effect. What sets her apart from the statue or the winged creature or those chatty cultists is that she's not *supposed* to be in the film. There's no mention of her in the script and, if you ask any number of crew members, Cross included, she doesn't exist.

"There it is," Cross says at the mention of his bogeywoman. "Like I said, you people don't care about my movie. It's always about her."

"You can't blame me for asking. The Sobbing Woman is as much a character as any other."

If you thought Cross was annoyed before, you should see him now. He shakes his head, like I'm a potty-training toddler struggling with the concept. "She's a *gag*. I don't know who she is or who dressed her up and I don't know how no one noticed until we had a cut of the film. But we were behind schedule. I was still editing two weeks before the premiere. There was no time for re-shoots. I figured at the very least, she added some atmosphere. And before you ask, yes, it's unfortunate that—"

"That she was spotted at the wrap party."

"That some *bitch* brought the costume along and played a prank, you mean."

"That's one way to put it."

It's not easy piecing together witness accounts from that night but when you do, it's clear they share a similar experience. I've spent the better—or worse, if you like—part of two years interviewing those present at the party.

To quote Geoff Stackton, one of the film's grips:

> Yeah, there was booze and some weed and more than a little coke, but it was nothing. We were unwinding after a shitty schedule. Went from having two months to three weeks. Studios, right? We were putting in twenty-hour days. So we partied there one last time as, like, a *fuck you* to the castle. That place is spooky as shit. We'd hear things at night. Footsteps and what sounded like something chewing with its mouth open. And that sobbing? We heard it, too. During production and especially the night of the party. We kept the coolers in the coat room. I stepped in there for a beer and the light went out. Whatever. I was on my sixth or seventh drink. Knew my way around by then. So I found the cooler, grabbed another one, and when I went to leave, the door slammed shut.
>
> 'Nice one,' I said. 'You guys can let me out now.' Figured someone was fucking with me. But the door wouldn't open and I started feeling like there was someone else in there with me. There was this smell, like rotten fruit or spoiled milk or *some*thing. And I swear I felt air on the back of my neck.

Warm air. Like a breath. Then I heard the crying. By the time I got out, Anna and Kimberly were already, you know...

Then there's Betty Frampton, the script supervisor, who stepped outside for a cigarette, and took cover under the front archway when she felt wetness on her forehead. She figured it had started to rain. But the liquid that dripped down her cheek was red, not clear. When she looked up, she saw viscous globs of blood leaking from the cracks between the stones. And who do you suppose she saw in the closest window, but a figure shrouded in a dirty dress and a veil?

Don't forget Brad Stetson, who played the role of Franky, the film's first victim. On screen, he meets his end by way of a sword through the heart. The suit of armor in one of Puzzle Point's—sorry, Holden Castle's—many parlors steps away from its corner and buries a blade deep within his rib cage.

The scene has sparked debate. Some viewers believe it was a mechanical booby trap, while others claim there's someone *inside* all that metal, perhaps the Sobbing Woman herself. But in reality, Franky—sorry, *Brad*—made it out of the wrap party unscathed. See, it was his grand idea to play hide and seek. If he hadn't, Kimberly and Anna wouldn't have hidden in a room that by all accounts does not exist.

Brad described a long, winding hall with sconces on either side. He recalled wondering who took the time to light those torches in the morning and snuff them at night, but what's less clear in his memory is the room where he found two of his co-stars.

It wasn't a door. It wasn't even, like, a door*way*. I just kept walking toward the sound of them whispering and then I was in this room. It's like the hallway just changed locations. When I looked behind me, I saw a spiral staircase leading down and I'm telling you, I didn't climb any steps. The room, it wasn't anything special. It wasn't anything at all. No furniture or shelves or whatever. It had these stained-glass windows but not like the kind you find in a church. Less Jesus and more things with too many limbs and wings. I saw them there—Anna and Kimberly, I mean. They were on the floor. Face down, thank god. But I was dumb enough to turn them over.

Brad said the flesh once housing their eyes, nose, and all the things that make up a face looked like raw hamburger. That's when he saw *her*. She stood in the corner, performing her signature water works, yet her face was contorted in what sure looked like a grin.

I could go on, but like Cross said, our interview's drawing toward its climax.

"You know what pisses me off the most?" He's standing now. He's also holding his steaming mug of coffee like he plans on scalding my face. "It's that they blamed *me* for some reason. It didn't happen on my watch. I was on a red eye by then, on my way to meet my editor."

"A director is to a film what a captain is to his ship. Ship goes down, it's on you."

"You read that on a bumper sticker?"

"They heard her that night, Mr. Cross. Some of them saw her, too."

"Don't," he says, pointing a finger, still clenching a cigarette, one that's burned down to the filter. It must be singeing his flesh but he doesn't seem to notice. That's too bad.

It's my turn to stand. Cross has a foot and a half on me but it's no different than bartending. He's just another asshole customer who thinks the world owes him a break.

What about me? Do I deserve a break?

That's what we came here to find out.

Sorry, that's what *I* came here to find out.

"Everyone always talks about Kimberly and Anna," I say, "but they weren't the only casualties."

"What're you talking about?"

"Alice Pearson, real name Alice *Kurtz*. She played Wanda in the film. Third to die. Tossed into a pit of snakes during snack time. Like that scene, she never really got out of Holden Castle. Not all of her. What she saw at the wrap party haunted her like Puzzle Point itself. She told me the Woman followed her home, took residence not in her bedroom, but in her *body*. Every night, she heard the sobbing. She tried white noise machines and fans. She tried ear plugs. Nothing drowned it out. The only thing that worked was stepping off the roof of her overpriced LA apartment building at approximately two-thirty-seven AM on August 12th, 1980, just one month before *Puzzle Point* was released. Paramedics said she died on impact, like that makes a difference. I'm sure you knew of her suicide but you don't know the *why*. You don't know it was because of a film you did as a favor. What you definitely don't know is that I write under a pen name. My last name is Kurtz. Alice was my sister."

I figure my confession will crack Cross, bring him to pathetic tears or at the very least humanize him in some capacity. But instead of *I'm so sorry* or *I'm begging you, please forgive me*, he says "Get out."

I don't.

"What if the Sobbing Woman was real? What if when you captured her on film, you—to put it bluntly—pissed her the hell off? Maybe she was fine living in the shadows and crying through those long nights in Holden Castle. Sorry, Puzzle Point. Because they're the same, aren't they? Films are reality and unreality. Once you say *action*, you create a copy of what's really there. That copy lives on."

"I'm calling the cops," Cross says, and with trembling

hands he sets down his coffee mug too hard, sends most of it spilling over the rim and onto the carpet. That's going to leave a nasty stain. He reaches for the rotary on his desk.

"It won't work," I say. What I don't say is *She won't let it.*

Cross slams the cradle a half-dozen times when the dial tone doesn't play nice. The plastic cracks, reveals wiry vasculature. He checks the phone line. Still plugged neat into the wall. Like I said, she's holding all calls.

"Out of my way," he says, even if there's three feet of distance between us. He heads for one of two doors in his office.

I could tell him the Sobbing Woman won't let him leave either but it's much too gratifying seeing the dread wash over him like a springtime thunderstorm. He tries the knob, which doesn't turn the slightest. Same goes for door number two.

"What the fuck did you do?" he says to me but he's asking himself the same question. Why couldn't he have just told Claudio *no*? He'd paid his dues by then, owed his mentor precisely nothing. *What the fuck,* indeed.

"What I did, Mr. Cross, is go to Puzzle Point for myself."

"You mean Holden Castle," he says, backing up until there's nowhere else to go.

"I went there for what you'd call closure. My sister had no history of depression or mental illness. Did you know she received a bachelor's degree in nursing from Salem State College? Our mother was a nurse before she retired early due to a stroke. Nurses are eternally overworked and yet Alice wanted to follow in Mom's droopy footsteps should her acting dreams not work out. And they didn't for a long time, unless you count commercials for tampons and dog food as stardom. But eventually, she auditioned for a certain film by a certain Italian genre director. She was a decent actress. With time and experience, she could've been a great one. But she was a better sister.

"What I did was sneak past security. From there it wasn't hard. Not like Holden himself is keeping watch. He's too busy doing whatever it is paranoid recluses do in their free time. He probably knows all about the Sobbing Woman. Maybe that's why he agreed to the shoot. Maybe he thought he could get rid of her that way.

"It felt like stepping into your little film. Because the set dressings were still there, like your crew never got around to tearing them down. The suit of armor, the altar, the subterranean chamber—all intact."

"That's not possible," Cross says.

"I can't argue with that. You know where I found her? In the dining room, just sitting at a table made to seat twenty but usually seats just one. She had her head in her hands and yes, she was sobbing. But it seemed like she didn't *want* to. It seemed like she was tired of crying. I told her I'd come to kill her or exorcise her or whatever you do to things that have stopped breathing yet won't die. I said I was Alice's sister, that I'd come for revenge or something close to it. And you know what *she* said? She said, 'I can help you.' And that's what she did."

The lights flicker. The room tremors. One might blame it on a California quake if they didn't know better.

But we know better.

"She only caught a ride with Alice that day to get to *you*. But Alice has always been stronger than me. She wouldn't give in."

I open my mouth and release a wracking sob not my own. The pressure in my chest is like being torn apart by an ever-growing tumor. I feel her climbing up my esophagus, feel her enter my throat, and then out she comes, dribbling down my chin in all her ectoplasmic glory. She starts as a puddle on the floor, a puddle that gains mass until it takes on the shape of a veiled woman. I wipe away the bits of her that didn't reform. It tastes like sour milk but I don't mind.

Cross may or may not notice that the walls of his office are more like stone now, stone that bleeds every now and then from its cracks. And the sole window looks out not at the Hollywood hills but at a red moon so full, it's a like a scene shot day-for-night. He may or may not sense that we've traveled from one coast to another without ever stepping on a plane. But what he notices for certain is the Sobbing Woman as she closes the distance between them and gets to work.

I step on something, feel it snap beneath my shoes. It's the review of *The Horror at Puzzle Point*, the glass fissured. A new frame is in order.

Consider it a business expense. I bring it with me on my way out.

That article's not going to write itself.

FUNERAL TRAIN

Matthew M. Bartlett

As the lights above the platform extinguished themselves one by one, despair wrapped skeletal fingers around the heart of Wendell Merntz. When he'd headed back to the station from the meeting, he was overconfident of his memory of the route and had gotten hopelessly lost in a tangle of identical-looking streets. By the time he finally spotted the glow of the station between two darkened mansions on the other side of a broad boulevard, he was too exasperated and exhausted to find much cheer in the discovery. But he'd hefted his suitcase with a sigh and headed in that direction. Once his shoes had gotten a thorough soaking after he'd gingerly attempted to cross a shallow brook, once his face had been scratched from forehead to chin by thorns, he'd finally located and climbed the concrete steps to the station.

Onto the glass-covered corkboard outside the doors was thumbtacked a printed schedule, which he inspected by penlight. It confirmed that the last train had come and gone. The next wouldn't come until morning: more than seven hours hence. The lack of light in all directions indicated that lodging, even if he could afford it, was a considerable walk away, and by this time he had no legs for walking.

He considered attempting to sleep on one of the benches, his back be damned, but when he walked over, he discovered that they had been fitted with dividers to prevent reclining. Wincing, cursing the conceiver, and, of course, the installer, of that cruel and diabolical obstruction, he shuffled back to the staircase that led down to the street. Perhaps, he thought self-pityingly, he could locate a hedge behind which to rest.

But then a distant whistle pealed. Merntz turned and rushed back to the platform, where he peered down the track. A wavering light flickered back where the rail curved into the forested land that bracketed it.

What was this? An unscheduled train? Perhaps a private conveyance, as for a wedding, or one hired by some nocturnal concern, private or municipal. No matter. It was headed in the right direction, and Merntz would proceed as far as he could toward home. At the very least, it might get him closer to a more densely populated area. Closer, maybe, to a hotel.

Did one hail trains? Was that done? What, Merntz wondered, was the protocol?

Now the light spread over the rail line, and he could hear the chugging of the wheels. A warm wind redolent of burning oil preceded the train, assailing Merntz's nostrils and pushing back his silver-black hair. When the locomotive finally resolved tall and imposing from the darkness, Merntz was startled at how closely it resembled the model trains of his youth. Giant twin spatulas, black and shining, formed a wedge at the front; above that, the coal-black face of the train brought to mind the door of a giant safe, the sort behind which a bank would keep its valuable documents. A smaller, silver circle sat atop that one, gong-like. The roof of the thing was a mishmash of smokestacks, domes, cupolas, and cylinders.

He leaned out, raised his chubby pink hand, and waved frantically.

At first, he thought the train would pass him by. It did

not decelerate; in fact, it appeared to be speeding up, as though to leave the station and the desperate man in its wake with pointedly impudent expedience. But then came the shrill, pandemonic, disjointed chorus of shrieking brakes, and before he knew it, a chain of passenger cars rumbled by him, finally stopping so that an entrance yawned exactly before where he stood. Relieved and yet fearing that they might decide to lurch away and leave him behind as some kind of cruel joke, he placed his hand on the steep railing and ascended into the lamplit gangway.

Merntz dragged his case down the aisle. He noticed right away an abundance of children. Every passenger or pair of passengers had a child with them. Oddly, none of the children were sleeping, despite the late hour. They all were on their best behavior, thankfully, even the very young ones. They sat quietly, hands folded in their laps. The parents were awake as well. All were dressed as for some formal event. Surely, then, this wasn't a funeral train nor any ordinary train: quite opposed to the somnambulant atmosphere he would have expected on any typical late-night run, there seemed to be excitement—or, at the very least, buzzing anticipation—in the air.

Merntz chose an empty seat near the back of the passenger car. He jammed his case into the overhead compartment. Nestling his ample bottom into the welcoming cushion, he finally allowed himself to feel something approaching contentment. He considered the meeting from which he'd come. It had been a resounding success. The firm let him know that over the past few days they'd abruptly terminated several powerful figures in their organization, figures resistant to change. This move, which Merntz and his partners had not anticipated, showed the firm's commitment to what would amount to a significant shift. At the close of the meeting, bonhomie and boozy conviviality abounded; business cards traded hands in great proliferation. Then, finally, handshakes all around, men lighting one another's pipes amidst agreement that a merger would be a boon to both parties. Formalities would be dispensed with and documents drawn up with alacrity. Merntz looked forward to informing his superiors, looked *very much* forward to reaping the rewards of his efforts as emissary.

Across the aisle sat a young woman in a hat with an expansive, fringed brim. A slight smile shone in her eyes; her mouth, offset by very pale flesh, was preternaturally small, even accentuated, as it was, with blood-red lipstick. Next to her sat rigid and upright a boy of about nine years, in a vest and fat little tie, his hair combed neatly, not a stray strand, the part as clean as a newly paved road. Their noses bore an identical elegant slope—only the size differed. In the spirit of nocturnal travelers' camaraderie, he smiled and nodded in their direction, but, despite the boy's sidelong glance, they did not acknowledge him.

On the seat next to him lay a folded newspaper. Good—something to pass the time. He started when he recognized the man in the photograph accompanying the lead story. Even with his aged, corrugated face and his bruised fingers, he was unmistakable. Very old, very thin, clad in a grey suit, he was being helped down courthouse steps by a coterie of young women insect-like in large black sunglasses, with long black hair, and clad in short, shining black raincoats over bare legs. The headline blared POPE SEVENIUS DEAD AT 99.

Merntz had at first known him by a different name: Pembroke. Whether that was a first name or surname, he hadn't known. Pembroke stood among the top brass in some of the group photos that graced the office walls. He was known in corporate circles—a level or two above Merntz's pay grade—as a political gadfly, a donor to politicians of every stripe, every persuasion, even those with competing ideologies. In news magazines and on the dealership television where Merntz brought his car to be serviced were pictures of the man seated at banquet tables with presidents; standing on red carpets with his bony hands on the shoulders of movie stars; at exclusive gatherings with poets and authors, prizewinners and laureates; head bowed in prayer with religious leaders. Merntz recalled in particular that crooked, sinister smile, the same expression in every picture, as though copied and pasted.

Merntz had also been privy to the exaggerations and bizarre claims—diabolism, devilish deformities, wanton slaughter, cannibalism—discussed clandestinely after meetings, over highballs and cigars at hotel bars, or in shaded conference center alcoves. He'd discounted the chatter as the lurid fantasies of terminally bored businessmen.

It turned out the truth was still quite hideous, even absent the fantastical embellishments. One night, a year or so ago, during his online meanderings, Merntz had stumbled onto a YouTube video in which a self-styled investigator exposed Pembroke's true identity: that of Pope Sevenius, prolific child murderer and sadist. For more than a decade the self-monikered Pope had reveled undetected in his dark work. The bodies of his victims—all children—were found in plastic garbage bags, often on the grounds of police stations or courtrooms. They were skeletons from the rib cage up. There was relief among some when forensic examination determined that the children had not been subjected to outrages born of prurience. But this was small comfort considering the accounts uncovered in the Pope's diaries upon his apprehension. Alongside heretical musings, fiendishly ribald rhapsodies, poor attempts at poetry, and incoherent passages of off-putting length were interminable and hideous accounts of torture and mutilation.

The video included footage of the press conference—fat sheriffs and exhausted looking officials crowding a microphone before a rabid press—and demonic courtroom sketches of the leering, sneering Pope. After a week-long trial, he was convicted on a stunning ninety-eight counts. He was subsequently sentenced to just seventeen years of incarceration, the brazen laxity of which provoked not only mass protests, but also threats and physical attacks against the judge and members of the jury, perpetrated by the victims' family members, the general public, and even the Pope's numerous devotees, who were outraged that he'd been convicted in the first place.

According to the YouTuber's breathless account, the Pope managed to immediately gather a circle of followers in prison despite his crimes, the specifics of which tend typically to make the perpetrator very much a pariah, or a target of all and sundry. Within weeks of his incarceration there were disappearances *from within the prison* of guards, fellow prisoners, and even, on one storm-stricken night, the prison warden himself. Soon after, Sevenius was released without fanfare, under cover of moonless dark, picked up by a black limousine and ferried away to no one knew where. His incarceration had lasted less than six months.

Surprising to precisely no one was the resumption of the disappearances of children almost immediately upon his release. Some of the bereaved families were targets of police investigations, suspected of being, if not instrumental in the kidnappings, complicit in some sort of unholy arrangement. All were vindicated, despite voluminous evidence. Through all this not a word was heard from the Pope. The house in which he'd lived prior to his imprisonment, an unassuming bungalow on a nondescript street, was set upon by an angry mob, which found little left to destroy. The house had been cleaned out to the walls and to the rafters. Strangely, the house refused to burn, despite the incandescent insistence of their torches and accelerants.

It was a decade later that he reappeared in public, his new name the only attempt to disguise his identity.

And now he was dead, the target of an assassin. According to the newspaper, he been attending an exclusive gathering not far, in fact, from the location of Merntz's meeting, and a man disguised as a servant leaned in to light the Pope's cigarette with what turned out to be an exploding lighter. Half the Pope's head was blown to powdered bone and sprayed flesh and brains. Four of the women with whom he was talking were also killed in the blast. The assassin's arm was blown off at the elbow. He might have survived, had not the Pope's acolytes and bodyguards set upon the fallen assassin, tearing him quite literally to shreds. His eyes and tongue were eaten, along with the tip of his nose and his earlobes.

The article focused on the violent assassination and its aftermath, then meandered in speculation regarding the Pope's connections to the powerful and well-known, names dropped like manure from the backside of a horse, the writer flirting with libel and making only fleeting mention of the vague "legal troubles" that had hounded Sevenius throughout his early years. The end of the article caused Merntz to gasp, for it revealed that the body of the Pope and his murdered crew were being transported on the very train in which Merntz was now a passenger.

Sudden discomfort twisted Merntz's belly and shot fireworks in his brain. He rose with the insistent idea of locating a porter and arranging for payment. Dropping the newspaper on the seat, he stood and pivoted into the aisle to find a man blocking his way, hands gripping the backs of the seats, forming a blockade. The man wore a scarlet trilby with a crumpled yellow flower in the band, a monocle, and a wet, loathsome grimace framed by a bombazine black Van Dyke beard shiny with gel. A badge above his breast pocket read GLOWERY. In a slinky voice with a vaguely European accent he said "Sir, what are you doing on this train?"

Merntz felt immediately guilty, but quickly recovered his senses. He was no stowaway or fare-dodger—he had every right to be here. "I was not stopped when I entered," he said. "No sign nor attendant was present to indicate any kind of exclusivity. In any event," he continued, patting his pockets, "I am able to pay any fare required of me, and happy to do so."

"Sir, you cannot be on this train."

"Well then, you may deposit me at the next station."

"I believe I shall expel you sooner than that," Glowery said, violence in his voice as he reached out hairy, fat-fingered hands toward Merntz's shoulders.

But then sudden light illuminated Glowery's face, and he froze. He looked past Merntz, out the window. A lighted sign floated by the train windows, the letters appearing one-by-one in each:

| L | E | E | D | S |

When the light from the sign slid away, it was supplanted by the eerie, shimmering orange-red of firelight glimmering and glowing in the trees. Here and there stood curious black tents the size of houses, billowing in the breezes. A muffled sound came from all around the train. High-pitched voices in ecstatic ululation. The passengers were standing now, entering the aisle, turning toward the back of the passenger car. Their faces were rapt with ecstatic joy and their lips trembled as they too loosed their terrible song into the compartment.

The door at the back blew apart, sending wood and glass flying. Merntz and Glowery raised their arms to protect their faces. From the billowing cloud of red ash and debris stumbled a creature with a face that bore the likeness of the man on the cover of the newspaper—the part of the face that remained. The thing was tall. It was lean. It was scored with countless scars. At its hind whipped a tail like a rolled-up and tapered relief map of the screaming faces of children. Another face, profusely pimpled and vicious, gibbered and drooled and panted where the spindly legs met. From behind this horrid thing lurched four women, blood-spattered, the flesh and muscle of their faces reduced to dangling ribbons.

This was a funeral train after all. Or, rather, Merntz thought, madness percolating in his stunned brain, *a resurrection train!*

The mother across the aisle burst from her seat, snatched up her boy, and pushed past Mertz and Glowery, knocking them into vacant seats as she rushed the child to the hideous Pope. Quick as a frog's tongue, the Pope snatched the child's leg just below the knee and tore him from his mother's arms. The child's shin bone snapped with a loud report; the boy now dangled awkwardly in that terrible grasp. His agonized shrieks tore through Merntz's ears, cutting off when the thing reaffirmed its grip and lifted the boy by his torso, digging its grotesque, misshapen mouth into the side of his head.

Merntz turned away in revulsion, only to see the mother kneeling in the aisle, her face essaying not horror, not grief, but exultation.

One of the Pope's undead acolytes leapt forward and flung the woman by the neck over the seats and into the window, glass and bone cracking. The door at the front of the passenger compartment slammed open and more passengers charged through, hefting children by their armpits. The children reached out for the hideous thing, begging to be taken. The parents pleaded, too. The Pope swept by Merntz and Glowery and waded into the crowd, tearing heads free from straining necks, peeling flesh from faces, necks, and arms, cramming everything into his foul, rotten mouth, gnashing and tearing with sharp brown teeth. A gust of foul wind assailed Merntz's nostrils, and he stirred from his stunned paralysis.

He bolted into the aisle and fled through the gaping, splintered maw from which the Pope and his witches had come. Past ruined seats and over peeled-up flooring he clambered, until he stumbled out between the cars.

The night rumbled by, tall grasses, wind that smelt of burning timber, a moving wall of trees a few yards away. Merntz, never a bold nor adventuresome man, crouched, hesitated...and then launched himself from the train. His arm glanced against the wheels as he flailed down, cracking his skull on the tracks, and rolled for several painful yards on rough gravel.

He lay for a minute as the sounds of the funeral train—the churning wheels, the agonized screams—sailed off into the illimitable night. Finally, silence, except for the chirping of crickets and the distant snapping and popping of burning wood. His breathing calmed. His head pulsed painfully in time with his heartbeat. Cautiously, gingerly, he inventoried his bones and muscles and attempted to climb to his feet. Dizziness and nausea overtook him. The world swam and pitched. He sat back down.

He tried again. A little better this time. Stretching his arms out for balance, his head still throbbing mightily, Merntz waded into the tall grass, heading for the tree line. A faint glow showed somewhere back in there, but he couldn't tell how far. He did not want to get lost in these woods.

Somewhere in his search for safety and civilization, he got rather turned around. The trees thickened as though closing ranks to expel him from their midst. Finally, he emerged onto an expanse of flattened grass. The train tracks appeared before him again like a long, fallen ladder, and he could not for the life of him discern in which direction that train had gone. He chose at random, and followed the tracks until he saw stoplights in the distance. As he walked, they just seemed to get farther away.

Eventually he found himself standing on the pavement below them. To his left, the road continued past dark Victorian and Dutch Colonial houses. To his right, a little up the silent road, crouched a closed convenience store, its wares dimly illuminated by security lights. Beyond that, a sign announced the presence of an establishment called The Cat's Fang, whose logo was a curved white tooth on a field of yellow. An electronic marquee below promised billiards, beer, and cocktails.

Just the thing. A celebratory drink, maybe another two or three non-celebratory ones to blot out the memory of the horrors of the train, and then perhaps a server or a patron might be able point the way to a place where he could bed down for the night.

The bar was a squat little building with iron bars protecting narrow horizontal windows. When Merntz opened the door, his way was blocked by two men in black suits, thick-set goons with slicked-back black hair and mirrored sunglasses. Spiraling red wires led from their earpieces to behind their lapels. They looked him over, grinned great, false shark grins, and separated to let him pass. The interior was lit only by strung-up multicolored lights, Keno games, and several widescreen televisions, all showing news coverage of Pope Sevenius's assassination.

Merntz groaned and beelined for the mostly unpopulated barstools. A cadaver stepped into his path. It was a woman, one of the Pope's women from the train. One mangled breast hung out from where her raincoat had melted away. It was red and bubbly like a rooster's wattle. She flashed three teeth at him in an attempt at a smile, and reached out an unmarred hand—soft, pale flesh, long fingers, impeccably painted red nails.

It was perhaps the most beautiful hand Merntz had ever seen. It looked soft, too. He was almost afraid to touch it. But he reached out and she took his hand in hers. It was very, very cold. She brought him to a corner table partially encircled by a curved oak bench. There, the dead Pope Sevenius sat between two dead women. The table stank of charred flesh, stale beer, ashes, and perfume. Another dead woman lolled to the Pope's right, a half blown-out eye twitching in its charred socket. At the Pope's direction, Merntz slid into the booth next to her, and the one who'd led him over sat next to him. Once he was between them, they edged over til their hips touched his, and they cooed and ruffled his hair.

Before the Pope sat a sheaf of papers half as tall as the pint glass next to them. Pope Sevenius lay a singed hand atop it.

"Your new partners failed to convince me of the efficacy of a merger," he said in a voice like a snake's hiss. "They attempted to *dismiss* me. They have found that I am not so easily dismissed. So I'm starting my own venture. I'm here tonight in the capacity of executive recruiter."

He smiled grotesquely from that ruined face. Merntz gulped.

"Look it over," said the Pope. "We have all the time in the world."

"Let's order you a drink," said the dead woman to Merntz's left in a gore-gargling baritone. "To celebrate. What's your poison?"

...ED É QUI, NEL FIUME DI SANGUE...CHE TROVERAI LA VERITÀ CHE VAI CERCANDO...
(...AND IT IS HERE, IN THE RIVER OF BLOOD...THAT YOU WILL FIND THE TRUTH YOU SEEK...)

doungjai gam

A cry pierced the silence of the night—low, sharp, startled.

Mariangela blinked as she sat up and looked around. The night and all its eeriness draped over the house like a thick blanket, warm and suffocating. Beside her, Bruno slept like the dead.

Again she heard the cry, louder and full of fear.

Silvia.

She crept out of the bedroom and across the hall. The door groaned in protest as Mariangela pushed it open. In darkness, the child's slight frame was undetectable beneath the layers of blankets and stuffed animals strewn across the canopy bed. She stepped closer, anxious: *Has she fallen back asleep? Was I hearing things?*

A whimper: *mama?*

Relief washed over Mariangela.

"Yes, my baby. Mama is here." She sat on the edge of the bed, running her hand over the fleece blanket and rubbing Silvia's thin legs. Her daughter's cries became shriller.

"Shh, my dear. Let's not wake your daddy up." She laid next to her and reached out to smooth Silvia's hair. She pulled the blanket away to reveal a skull staring back at her, maggots spilling from the eye sockets.

"*Nooooo!*"

Mariangela stood awkwardly and lost her footing, stumbling and grunting as she backed into the canopy post. She gasped in pain as she rubbed her lower back.

The sudden jolt forced the skull into motion—it rolled off the pillow, struck the corner of the nightstand and hit the floor to roll towards Mariangela, a trail of writhing maggots in its wake. She continued screaming but could still hear the echo of her daughter calling for her.

mamamamamamamamamamamamama

Behind her, the door slammed open. Silvia's cries reverberated in her head, loud and unrelenting.

mamamamamamamamamamamamama

Everything was spinning. Mariangela couldn't tell if it was the room, the house, or just herself. The skull hit her foot and came to a halt. The jawbone broke off, clattering against the hardwood. The piles of maggots grew as they squirmed closer to her. She tried to sweep them away with her naked foot.

mamamamamamamamamamamamama

The world around her became a bold, blue panic. One uncertain step begat another as she reached for something, anything to keep her steady.

She shook wildly—no, she was being shaken. A sharp sting to her face brought her back to reality. Blue panic was replaced by sobering darkness, the floor beneath her solid once more, the angry face of Bruno so close to hers that his mustache hairs tickled her upper lip.

"What are you doing?"

She wanted to answer him, but she couldn't summon the words.

Mariangela awoke while Bruno was getting ready for work. After their late-night confrontation, she had no desire for another, so she lay in silence with her eyes closed. Before he left, he stood over her and she felt the heat of his glare. She kept her breathing steady until she was sure he had left the house, leaving the bed only after the Mercedes started up and tore down the road.

Another day of Bruno arriving to work late, another reason for him to dislike her.

She went about her morning routine, taking care to avoid Silvia's bedroom. Bruno's sister and her family were coming for the weekend, and she'd fallen behind on getting the house ready. After she hung the bed sheets on the clothesline, she drove into town to run errands. On the way home, she slowed as she drove by the cemetery.

mama

Mariangela shut her eyes and gripped the steering wheel, her foot holding the brake pedal to the floor.

I have to get ready for tonight, for the weekend.

mama, please

Behind her, a couple in a convertible shouted as the driver honked the horn. As they drove around her, the driver made a face and extended his middle finger while his much younger and more attractive passenger pointed and laughed. Mariangela tried to ignore their leering faces as she made the turn into Saint Agnes Cemetery.

Silvia was tucked away in a back corner far off the main path, her grave under a maple tree with a view of the Harbinger River. The graveyard was deserted but Mariangela locked her car door anyway. As she walked through rows of grass and granite, she tried to forget the events of the night before.

Though she visited daily, the sight of her daughter's final resting place choked her up every time. The headstone itself was nothing impressive. It was made of marble with her name and dates etched upon its surface. What was unusual was the set of six steps that led down into the earth. At the landing there was a viewing window above Silvia's head.

In their initial grieving period, Bruno had given Mariangela free reign on the burial plans, but once he saw the costs skyrocketing, he quickly stepped in with his objections. No, Silvia did not need a set of matching flower urns on either side of the headstone. No, they did not need an elaborate marble bench under the maple tree for them to sit and endlessly grieve over their only child. And for godssakes, why would they bother with a family mausoleum? *What if we move away? Who would come to visit us after we're gone?*

That he had agreed to the steps and the viewing window was inconceivable, but getting him to compromise took an onslaught of tears, a bottle of pills, and a trip to the hospital. She also agreed to use some of the inheritance money from her mother to pay for those extras.

Bruno found the whole arrangement distasteful and visited twice a year at most. Mariangela made it a point to visit daily, as the cemetery was only a couple of miles from home.

As she approached, she paused and took a deep breath before putting on a sad smile.

"My sweet, sweet Silvia," she said as she took the first two steps down and sat on the ledge that ran the perimeter of the grave. She clutched a copy of Silvia's favorite book, *Little Red Riding Hood*. The well-loved copy they used to read every night was at home on the nightstand; this was one of a handful of books of nursery rhymes and fairy tales that Mariangela kept in her car to read to Silvia when she visited.

The cold stone chilled her. Autumn was approaching fast. She placed the book on her lap and let it fall open. With a tremor in her voice, she began to read: "Once upon a time, there was a little girl..."

She continued on, not noticing the sky drift from a cheerful blue to dismal grey. The wind picked up a few times and turned the book's pages prematurely. It was only when she felt the first few sprinkles of rain that she remembered the bed sheets hanging on the clothesline and the groceries in the trunk. She cursed under her breath as she stood. She took a few more steps down and looked into the window.

Instead of Silvia's cherub face and flaxen hair, there was only rotting flesh and maggots getting their fill.

Mariangela screamed and turned to retreat but instead she tumbled and fell forward, her ribs crashing against the top step, her left palm bloodied from scraping against the stone. She stood and brushed the dirt from her coat. She found a used tissue in her pocket and clutched it, trying to ignore the pain. She was ready to leave when she realized that the book was missing. She looked around in a mild state of panic.

There was no sign of it anywhere.

She peered down the stairs. The book rested over the viewing window. The thought of seeing the decay again unnerved her, but she couldn't leave the book there, especially with a storm coming. She stepped down carefully, using the ledge to keep her steady. She picked the book up, sighing with relief when she saw her angel daughter's perfect visage, unmarred by rot and feeding creatures.

Raindrops pelted her, hard, fast, and cold.

"The bed sheets!" Bruno would be so upset with her.

She made her way out of the grave and hurried to the car.

The sheets were damp, so she draped them over the doors and radiators with the hopes they would be dry by nightfall. They were the least of her worries—there was still much cleaning and cooking before Sophia arrived with her husband and twins in tow. She dreaded their visits but kept her mouth shut. It wasn't like she would be able to get a word in edgewise, anyway.

Their guests arrived earlier than expected and Bruno was nowhere to be found, so it was up to Mariangela to entertain them while making sure dinner didn't get ruined. Sophia and Ivan kept her company in the kitchen while the twins ran roughshod through the house with their German Shepard, Zeus. She was sure that Bruno would be outraged about the extra furry guest—he hated animals, to the point where he had denied Silvia even a beta fish.

Bruno came in as she was pulling the chicken from the oven.

"Mariangela, why are the sheets—oh, Sophia!" He greeted his sister with a gusto his wife never experienced. After many hugs and kisses and even an affectionate pat on the head for Zeus, he turned to Mariangela.

"This place is a mess! Why is dinner not ready?"

"It's almost ready," she muttered.

"*It's almost rea-dee, it's almost rea-dee!*" the twins chanted as they ran outside after Zeus.

Sophia placed her hand on Bruno's shoulder. "Your wife has had a long day. Come, take your jacket off and let's go sit. We have much to catch up on." The fire in his eyes faded.

"Everything smells good," he mumbled as his sister led him away.

Ivan lingered behind, watching Mariangela's every move.

"Do you need any help?"

"No, thank you. I'll have everything on the table in a moment." She reached for a bowl in the cupboard, nearly dropping it when she felt Ivan at her back. He slid his arms around her waist and she stiffened, grimacing in pain from her earlier fall.

"It's so good to see you again," he whispered in her ear. He kissed her neck, and she cringed as she felt one of his hands moving towards her bosom.

Behind them, the sliding door opened, and she stomped on his big toe. He yelped and backed away as Lucia and Daria came running in with Zeus, all of them rain-soaked. Zeus shook himself dry and the girls followed suit, giggling all the while. Ivan scowled at her before turning away.

"Come, children, you both need to get dried off—Auntie has prepared us a fabulous feast!" He shooed them out of the kitchen. He turned back and grinned cruelly at her.

Considering the events of the day, Mariangela thought that dinner had come together well. Sophia naturally had her own opinions: the chicken was tough, the potatoes not quite cooked through. She made a point of using salt before every other bite. She spoke over everyone and for everyone. When Bruno asked his nieces about school, Sophia would chime in first about their grades, which one was better at what subject, and so on. Lucia and Daria ate their spaghetti in silence, with Zeus at their feet. Ivan tried to recompense for his earlier indiscretion by complimenting the meal, but Sophia kept coming back with retorts about the dryness, the burnt bits. He too fell quiet as Sophia and Bruno dominated the conversation.

Outside, the rain continued, occasionally punctuated by thunder. The twins squealed with glee whenever the lights flickered.

Mariangela tried her best to keep a pleasant face on while gritting her teeth. She cleared most of the dinner plates, rejecting Ivan's offers of help, and poured coffee for the adults. She brought in cream and sugar, gripping the bowl handles so tightly she thought they might break. The twins were eager for cherry pie despite not finishing their dinner. While Mariangela was getting the dessert plates and silverware, screams echoed from the dining room. She rushed back, her hands full.

The cherry pie, which had been sitting in the middle of the table cooling over the course of dinner, had burst open. The contents, impossibly red and viscous, were splattered across the white tablecloth. Daria and Lucia stared at each other wide-eyed as they picked bits of cherry from each other's hair. Ivan stood up, the front of his pants a crimson mess. He tried to blot the stain with a napkin and some water but that made it worse. Sophia's eyes were glassed over; the events had shocked her into a rare moment of silence. Bruno glared at Mariangela.

Sophia gasped and pointed at the pie, which had begun jiggling. Pairs of spindly legs rose from the cherry goo, followed by a head and body that seemed too big to be real. Once the spider was fully free, its back exploded and the babies scattered across the table.

Mariangela screamed and dropped the dishes. Daria and Lucia shrieked as they ran upstairs to safety while Zeus barked at nothing and everything at once. Ivan crushed spiders one by one with his napkin until Sophia shoved him out of the way and grabbed at the tablecloth, trying to ball it up.

The mother spider latched onto Sophia's wrist, its mandibles tearing at her flesh. She screamed, slamming the creature against the table—it took three tries for the spider to release her grip and curl into a ball, dead. Bruno grabbed his half-eaten drumstick and beat the spider to a pulp while Sophia seized the bundled-up tablecloth and ran into the kitchen, pushing Mariangela out of the way, not mindful of the broken dishes underfoot. Blood spatter trailed behind her like breadcrumbs as she raced onto the porch and threw what remained of dinner into the backyard. She stormed back to Mariangela and shook her bloody wrist at her.

"What kind of a joke is this?" she yelled, crimson droplets spattering on the walls and floor. She walked away cursing, with the men scampering behind her.

Mariangela sank to the floor and wept.

She spent the rest of the evening alone, cleaning up the broken dishes and the blood of her sister-in-law. Zeus padded through a couple of times to check for food scraps and a pat on the head, and she happily obliged. The twins came downstairs for the bed sheets and left after getting a glass of milk and a hug from their aunt. The walls and floor needed a more thorough scrubbing, but it could be finished in the morning. To reward herself, she stood by the back door and lit a cigarette. When Silvia received her diagnosis, she and Bruno had made a pact to quit smoking. They both picked it back up after she died.

She exhaled, blowing the smoke through the screen. Three years since Silvia took her last breath, alone in a hospital bed and hooked up to machines that emphasized her smallness, her fragility. Mariangela had kept a bedside vigil, but the one moment she walked away to use the restroom...

She leaned against the door frame, sobbing. She

started to close the sliding door, ready to crush her cigarette when she heard a whimper and felt a wet nose.

"You want to go outside, sweetie?"

Zeus bounded into the darkness while she stood under the awning and continued to smoke. The rain hadn't let up, but Zeus paid no mind as he wandered the yard, marking his territory.

In the distance, a loud crash startled them. Zeus stopped in front of her and stared at the side of the house, as if expecting someone to come around the corner. Teeth bared, he was ready to pounce. She wiped her eyes and took a step closer, but nothing looked out of sorts.

"Zeus, come."

He growled and barked once, a warning.

"Zeus!" She reached for his collar and he snapped at her. She backed away from the dog and into someone, gasping as she turned to find Ivan behind her.

"I heard the dog. I didn't realize he was outside." A flash of lightning illuminated his eyes.

"I—I was just cleaning up and he wanted to go out."

Ivan snapped his fingers. "Zeus, come." This time the dog listened, trotted by them, and shook himself dry in the kitchen before wandering further into the house.

"How is Sophia's wrist?" She didn't care but figured it was polite to ask.

"We wrapped it up, it's fine." He waved it off as if it were no more than a splinter.

She offered him a drag and he accepted. They stood in silence and listened to the rain as they passed the cigarette back and forth. When he offered it back, he stepped in front of her and took her outstretched hand as he stubbed the cigarette in the ashtray next to her. She tried to ignore the fluttery feeling in her stomach. Ivan was a handsome man, tall and intimidating, with sharp cheekbones and a lethal combination of black hair and piercing blue eyes. But she was married, and that was that.

"Listen, I want to apologize for earlier. Sophia has no right to speak to you like that. Her and Bruno, they are alike. So rude and demanding."

"And are you any better than them with the way you acted earlier?"

He pretended to look stunned.

"Mariangela, I see how he treats you. You deserve better."

"Ivan, I—" He swooped in and silenced her with his lips. She struggled to get away, but he overpowered her, pinning her against the door. He wore only a thin pair of pajama bottoms, and she was aware of every inch of him. A soft moan escaped her lips as he caressed her breast and slowly thrust his hips.

The crash of thunder made them both jump, and he reluctantly let her go. She took advantage of the opportunity and slapped him.

"I love Bruno."

A lightning bolt lit up the sky and highlighted Ivan's features, now contorted in anger. He stormed past her, muttering. The only word she could make out from his rant was *whore*.

When she was sure he was gone, she slipped back inside and lit up another cigarette. As she blew smoke through the screen, she thought about what happened outside. Ivan was a bastard who couldn't keep his hands to himself, and she hated that for a fraction of a second, she enjoyed the way he held her. The way he kissed her. Why couldn't Bruno act like he loved her? She stretched her arms in front of her on the table and rested her head atop them.

mama, I thought you were going to quit.

She jerked up and looked around. There was a flash of white at the doorway. She blinked. Whatever it was, it was gone now.

Sighing, she crushed the cigarette and broke it in half. She threw it, along with the ceramic ashtray and the remainder of the pack, into the garbage.

At breakfast, Bruno announced he was bringing his sister's family to the zoo. When Mariangela declined to go, she wasn't shocked at his delight. She glanced at Ivan but he paid her no attention, instead focusing on the kids' table manners.

Within the hour, she had the house to herself. There was nothing of interest on the television so she put music on instead. She tried to distract herself by cleaning up the dining room. She made a face when she saw a chunk of spider she had missed when cleaning before breakfast. She used more napkins than necessary to wipe up the goopy mess. The rain had stopped during the night, so she threw the windows open for fresh air. She scrubbed the walls and floor with extra vigor.

Once finished, she turned off the radio and lay on the couch. The autumnal breeze chilled her. She wrapped herself in a throw blanket and, before long, drifted off to sleep.

When she awoke, it was cold and dark.

"Bruno?"

No one was around. Zeus didn't even come running. Surely he needed to be fed or let out.

"Zeus, come! Where are you?" She sat up and turned on a lamp—nothing. She tried another and got the same result. The damn power must have gone out again.

mama?

Mariangela turned toward the voice. Sitting near the bottom of the staircase with Zeus was her daughter.

"Silvia?"

She was in her burial dress, which—had she lived— would have been her communion dress. Her rhinestone tiara had a tulle veil attached in the back. The moonlight reflected off her patent leather shoes, shiny and brand new.

mama.

"Yes, my sweet angel?"

I miss you.

"I miss you so much." She choked back a sob.

mama. I need you to come visit me.

She stood and began walking, but Silvia held up a hand to halt her.

the river, mama. please come to the river.

please.

She took another step towards her daughter and then everything went black.

Mariangela woke up with a scream. Daylight and cold air poured in through the open windows. A glance at the clock confirmed that less than an hour had gone by since she passed out. She looked frantically around the room, but Silvia wasn't there. Her heart sank in disappointment that lingered like an unwanted guest.

The blanket had fallen away and Zeus took it upon himself to drag it by the loveseat and use it as a bed. She shivered as she shut the windows. After she closed the last one in the kitchen, she paused and stared outside. Tree branches littered the lawn, along with the tablecloth and broken dishware. She considered going out to clean it up but remembered the creature's babies—all dead now, surely, but still. She shuddered before walking away.

Moments later, a branch crashed through the window. Glass sprayed across the floor as she screamed.

mama!

Saint Agnes hadn't fared well during the storm. Downed

trees forced Mariangela to park closer to the entrance. Branches large and small, leaves, and trash from overturned garbage bins lay sprawled across the grounds. One tree had smashed a row of headstones on its way down, and she felt sorrow for the loved ones of the departed. In the distance, the maple standing over Silvia's grave was in terrible shape. She quickened her pace, dreading the worst.

As she approached, her fears were confirmed: lightning had hit the tree, causing an upper section to fall and knock over Silvia's headstone. A branch several feet in length was sticking up from the stairwell.

"No!"

She ran over. The branch had broken through the viewing window, shattering the glass. There was no sign of Silvia.

Mariangela fell to her knees and wept. Her heart hurt and she wondered if she could continue on. As she bawled, she thought she heard something nearby. She looked around, hoping no one was around to witness her embarrassing display.

"*Mama.*"

Before her stood Silvia, no longer the angel in white that she was the day of her burial. Her dress was torn and dirty, and the same could be said for the flesh on her hands. Her shoes were scuffed. Some of the rhinestones in her tiara were missing, her veil shredded. Her flaxen hair was streaked with mud.

"*Mama. Please bring me home.*"

Mariangela stood and wiped her tears away. She offered her hand.

"Of course, baby."

Silvia took her hand and they walked to the car in silence.

Dusk came and night followed.

It was after ten when Sophia's sedan roared into the driveway and went silent. Chattering voices carried through the night air. The twins had fallen asleep clutching stuffed animals. Their father and uncle carried them inside.

"Why are all the lights on?" Sophia complained as she stepped into the foyer. "Bruno, there's a draft in here."

"Quiet, Sophia, you'll wake the girls," Ivan said.

She laughed at him. "These girls will sleep through anything, unlike you." Bruno motioned for Ivan to follow him upstairs.

Sophia went into the kitchen for a drink and noticed the broken window. *It figures that woman would leave this for Bruno to fix. Mariangela is worthless.*

"Bruno! The window is broken!" She waited for his reply, but none came. She shivered as she got a glass of water and went upstairs.

After they put the twins to sleep in Silvia's room, they all decided it best to get some sleep themselves. Bruno promised his sister he would look at the window in the morning.

The bedroom was cold, as if there was a broken window in there, too. His wife was sound asleep, oblivious. He glared at the shape of her. He wanted to slap her for ruining this special weekend.

Before dawn, Bruno awoke to a noise. He rolled over and realized Mariangela wasn't in bed. He sat up, confused.

Another bark. That goddamned dog.

He got up and skulked into the hallway. What he really wanted to do was grab Ivan by the collar and tell him to keep his damn smelly dog in a kennel the next time they came over. His brother-in-law was a fool who fancied himself a ladies' man—he'd seen him hitting on his wife on more than one occasion, but Mariangela looked down her nose at him. For all her faults, she was loyal.

Bruno sighed. One more thing he would have to talk to Sophia about. She could do much better than that clown.

He was on the stairs when he heard giggling. He turned and looked but there was nothing. Maybe the girls were awake and entertaining themselves. He wistfully thought of his own daughter and wished that Silvia had been with them today to see the animals at the zoo. She loved the elephants and giraffes, and he'd promised her that one day after she was cured that they would go on a safari.

Sadness tried to overcome him, but he shook it off. One grieving fool in this house was more than enough.

The ground level was freezing. He sighed, thinking he should have found something to cover the window earlier. The tiles in the kitchen were like ice, and he wished he'd thought of putting his slippers on.

Mariangela sat in the shadows, her red-brown curls mussed up as if she hadn't brushed her hair in days. Zeus sat at her feet.

"Mariangela." She didn't acknowledge his presence. "What is this nonsense? What happened to the window?" He struggled to keep his voice at a whisper. "I am tired of your moping around the house." He continued without giving her a chance to respond. "You never want to go anywhere except the cemetery. Do you think Silvia knows or cares that you go to visit her every day? She's dead, Mariangela. Do you understand me?"

Mariangela stood and approached him. The light of dawn illuminated her pale flesh. Her eyes were two white orbs. A rivulet of blood trickled from her nostril. Bruno gasped and stepped back.

"What—what happened to you?"

She looked at the German Shepard, now at her side.

"Zeus, attack."

Bruno's face contorted from anger to fear as the dog

leapt and knocked him backwards. He expected to crash into the basement door, but instead found himself falling further away from his wife and the diminishing light. He hit the ground and was flooded with pain.

His left arm was underneath him in a way that didn't feel natural. He groaned; it hurt to breathe. He tried to raise his head and look up the stairs, but his neck was weak. Every bone felt broken.

"Mariangela, you bitch!" he cried out. Even speaking was painful.

She was a specter floating at the top of the stairs.

"Zeus." Her voice was cold. "Kill."

The dog pounced down the stairs.

She closed the basement door, muffling the brutal cacophony of Bruno's death.

"What is going on?"

She turned to find Ivan standing at the edge of the kitchen.

"Nothing." She backed away.

"That sounds very much like something." He reached for the doorknob. She grabbed his hand and led him deeper into the darkest corner of the kitchen.

"Mariangela—" She pressed her finger against his lips to shush him. She ran her fingertips lightly down his naked torso and tugged at the drawstring of his pajama pants, hoping to distract him from the sounds of dying in the basement. Eager, he helped her pull his pants down to his knees then guided her head to him. She tried not to gag at the overwhelming taste of piss as she took him in her mouth. He groaned in pleasure as he grabbed fistfuls of her hair and thrust himself harder, deeper...

And then came the pain. Ivan screamed as her teeth penetrated his skin. He flailed at her to no avail as he fell to the floor, writhing in pain.

She sat next to him, spat his cock out, and smiled at him. There was no sign of life—of anything—in her eyes.

"What—what the fuck," he yowled as she reached into

his newly-opened groin hole and yanked out a small length of intestine. The severed penis lay on the tile, blood spilling from both ends.

She stood and went to the basement door, where Zeus was scratching and whining. She opened the door and he came barreling out at Ivan.

Upstairs, a woman screamed. Mariangela followed the sound, leaving Zeus to feed on his former master.

Mariangela was near the top of the stairs when her foot bumped against something wet. She flipped the lights on to find Sophia lying on the landing with her neck snapped, her head resting on the step below. Blood spilled from the open wound on her throat and her empty eye sockets. Intestines and other organs were draped over the handrails. Crude, gory fingerpaintings decorated the walls.

The twins sat on either side of their mother's eviscerated torso. Lucia grabbed a freshly severed length of intestine, paying no mind to the contents spilling out. Daria held her mother's eyeballs, rolling them around in her hands like marbles. She handed one to her sister. They looked at the eyes, then at each other, before popping them into their mouths. Vitreous jelly squirted out from between their lips as they bit down. Meanwhile, Silvia sat at her aunt's feet, playing with what might have been a liver.

"Silvia," Mariangela whispered.

"*Mama!*" She dropped the organ as she stood, and it squelched under her foot as she made her way to the stairs, stepping over her aunt's remains.

Mother and daughter held hands. Mariangela wanted so badly to hug her baby, but feared she would crush her.

"Mama, can we go to the river?"

"Of course, sweetheart. Anything you want."

Lucia and Daria stood and followed them outside.

The skies were grey and threatening. They walked in pairs down the driveway and up the street, hands clasped together, unbreakable bonds. The fog was thick and impenetrable. What began as a drizzle turned into a downpour when they reached the cemetery gates.

Silvia led them to the far corner and the wreckage of her grave. The branch was still stuck in the depths beyond the viewing window, the stairwell filling with water. Beyond the stone fence, the Harbinger River was rising, its normally clear waters a deep red.

Mariangela climbed unsteadily over the rocks and stood at the riverbank. Unbeknownst to her, the twins had brought a length of their mother's intestines with them and were swinging it as if it were a jump rope. Silvia stood atop the stone fence holding a chunk of her fallen headstone. She threw it at her mother, striking her in the temple. There was no pain. She fell silently into the river and the waters surged in acceptance of its gift.

The girls backed away as the torrent grew, crimson spilling over the stone fence and permeating the grounds. The rain fell red and thick. Silvia and her cousins walked towards the front gate, waiting for their companions to join them.

A hand rose from the waters and grabbed a nearby rock. Mariangela emerged and clung to the rocks like moss.

All around the cemetery, the dead came forth. Corpses in varying states of decay shambled across the grass, the crowd slowly building as they joined the girls at the gate. Silvia stood tall, ready to lead them forward.

...and it is here, in the river of blood...that you will find the truth you seek...

Mariangela let go of the rocks and let the tide sweep her away.

DISCOTECA DE SANGUE (DISCO OF BLOOD – 1980)

Mer Whinery

Audio cassette tape found in an old tan Naugahyde suitcase at the estate sale of one Susann Korda of Sol Diablo, Texas. The combination lock looks to have been pried away with a chisel or screwdriver. Battered but in serviceable condition. Tape is a Memorex 90 High Bias cassette with the number 70, part 1 of 3, noted in smudged, faded black Sharpie. Case and contents purchased for two dollars, as is, with absolutely no returns allowed. There is the faint odor of stale marijuana smoke and dried beer clinging to the tacky red velvet fabric of the interior. The suitcase is empty except for the tape and a sheet of water-stained notebook paper, neatly folded, tucked beneath the tape.

The voice from the cassette, baptized in decayed hiss and dusty static pop, belongs to a man of age indeterminable. He speaks in a somnolent, honey-barbecued drawl. Every word drawn out as if in deliberation of each and every syllable and inflection. The tone of a man who enjoys his smokes and liquor and probably knows how to cook a mean rack of ribs. The cadence of a born storyteller who likes to purr dark fables into the ears of folks who like to listen.

They call me The Sorcerer, and I am a collector of tales. Tales of a very specific, ghoulish flavor which most folks with half a lick of sense would never believe, much less let slip past their lips and into the ear of someone else—unless they were drunk, high, or just flat-out off of their nut. This here tape, though, is a little something special. Here's why.

Most of the stories I have gathered over the years tend to revolve around the route I drive my old Peterbilt on. Mostly from Oklahoma, Texas, Missouri, and Arkansas. But every so often I motor out west and pick up a good whopper or three in Colorado or Nevada. California now and again. This tape is particular because it's the account of something in a specific spot that happened to more than one person. And the account in question didn't even happen in the USA. This one comes by way of Europe. Portugal to be exact. An old nightclub on the Rio Tejo known to all who have passed beyond its doors and lived to tell the tale as the *Discoteca de Sangue*. The Disco of Blood.

Can't resist a hook like that, can ya?

I have committed all of the stories regarding this here place told to me, these spookshows for the ears, onto tape for posterity. Just one tape, because I am a cheap son of a bitch and needed the bread for a pint of Old Raven rather than to buy more cassettes. Thinkin' outside the box there, hoss.

(A brief silence. Snap of microphone audio coming to life..)

The date is September 16th, 1980. This is the account of Jorge Grau, original owner of The Starlight Club in Lisbon, Portugal. Recorded at the Denny's in Rust River, Texas.

(A new voice takes over. An old man, bordering upon ancient. His coarse voice like sun-blistered leather and attic

dust. His heavily Spanish-inflected English is, however, quite good and easy to follow.)

I shouldn't have opened the club on that day. I think that might have been what caused all of these problems. But I am a Catholic still, despite my many vices and iniquities, and we tend to believe very strongly in the power of time and place. A baby born on Christmas Day is cursed to a life a misery or might actually transform into a goblin. Or a werewolf. An agent of Satanás. I opened the Club Starlight on November 1st, 1966. Dia de Todos los Santos...All Saints' Day. Maybe that's why the dead would not remain silent there. I offended them by building a place of pleasure upon a day meant for their reverence. Such things are of little significance when you are seeing gold glitter in the eyes of the face looking back at you in the mirror. But if I could go back now, I would have never laid a single brick on that cursed piece of earth. I should have razed it to the ground when I left it behind. I have to live with that, still. It is a guilt I will never be able to reconcile. I accept that I deserved this.

The problems started on opening night. That should have been my clue it was a doomed enterprise. It started small. So small you could not chalk it up to the damned nature of the land until months later when I had acquired perspective.

Let me preface this by telling you something about the soil upon which I built my misery, for it has bearing. I will be brief, as I only have a few hours before I must catch my bus. I had purchased the plot of land, totaling a little over two hectares, from a man whose life I had saved in the war and who felt he owed me a favor. I bought the land for a pittance, another red flag. I was told by many of the local laborers the ground was sacred to the Conquistadores who had inhabited what is now Lisbon, many centuries before. Allegedly a great, bloody conflict had been fought between the Conquistadores and a large knot of African slaves they had brought over from the dark continent. An uprising of some sort in which no man, woman, or child had been left standing. Indeed, while laying the foundation for the Starlight we unearthed many relics of war which could have only belonged to these Portuguese soldiers, as well as some relics I did not recognize.

Let me tell you, young man, I have been around the world many times over. I have laid my own hand upon the heathen standing stones in the English countryside. Drank cold beer on the steps of an Aztec jungle ruin. I have dipped these old, broken hands deep into the burning sand of the Sahara. I could tell immediately these artifacts were not African. Not of the Conquistador. These had come from someplace else. Someplace old and foul, having existed before men had been fashioned from clay and breathed to life by the Maker. You could actually feel it when you held these things in your hands.

But I didn't care. Of course I didn't. All I could see was the promise of the cash coming in and the beautiful, beautiful ladies dressed in their see-through silks and curve-fitted satin. Women unafraid to show their charms and offer their services at a high cost to men with too much money and a complete privation of moral fortitude. Yes, you heard that correctly, my burly friend. I was, and am, a man of many talents and I wore many hats. I like to call myself a man of connections. I brought people together for mutually beneficial transactions. But let us not mince words. I was a pimp. There is no way to describe it otherwise. But I was the best pimp to ever walk the streets of Lisbon, and while I reigned, I reigned supreme.

The Club Starlight opened on that hallowed night, as planned. I like to think of that moment as the match struck and applied to a long, slow-burning fuse. Within hours of opening our doors to a line of beautiful people stretching for almost half a mile, the fights began to break out. Now, men getting physical with one another in the presence of gorgeous ladies and under the witchcraft of strong alcohol was to be expected. But this was different. These incidents were more like savage dogs fighting in a dirty alleyway. A strange level of barbarism that left one man with many broken bones, another with a switchblade in his belly, and one poor woman minus an eye. But that was not the worst of it. The man who had plucked the eye from the face of the woman had held the poor soul down and forced her to watch him eat it. Her eye. Chewed it up like a grape and swallowed it. He had to be escorted from the club in restraints, of course. Cackling like a loon about things that did not make sense. You know, the sort of shit only loons find funny.

Now I understand the joke all too well.

Every other evening was a repeat of that grim opening night. You could count on at least one person leaving the club wounded, intoxicated to the verge of insensibility, or weeping over a romance gone sour. Although a popular, exciting place to be, it never really felt like a happy one. The police started to hang around a lot more than I would have desired. Not that it really hurt a specific branch of the business as much as you might think. They really don't care about that sort of thing over there like they do in America. Prudes in Public, Perverts in Private is how it works here. Yet I have discovered people tend to behave better when law enforcement is present, and if I have learned anything at all it is that people behaving themselves tend to not spend as much money as when they are allowed to be complete, unrepentant miscreants. But I was still making money. In fact, all through my association with the club I made money hand over fist. I know now it was the Devil's currency. My compensation for allowing his minions to prowl the glowing floors and gilded VIP rooms of the Starlight to spread his ghastly infection. I know now that when I built that damnable place I had opened a doorway leading straight into Hell.

So, building the club was my first mistake. The second mistake, possibly more catastrophic than the first one, was hiring her.

I didn't even question it when she came into my office that Sunday morning, just before closing time, demanding, not asking, that I give her a job. Not just any appointment, but a situation where she would be given the veritable keys to the kingdom. She wanted to manage the party girls, as I liked to call them. Perhaps it had been because of her incredible beauty I did this, along with her bewitching confidence. I felt as if I were being interviewed by her, and never once did I question this until it was all over. Even now, sitting here in this greasy, smelly place, I can still taste her light perfume of ginger and rosemary—and something vaguely savage. See the glints of white light from the dance floor mirror ball in the deep silhouette of her long hair and huge dark eyes. Her flesh pale as a freshly woven winding sheet and a smile that could command any man—or woman for that matter—to do her bidding without reservation no matter how absurd the request.

Adulphina was her name. Where she had come from I never knew. I never asked. All I know is that from the very second I saw her she was all I could ever think about afterwards. This was not a good thing to have happen to me, mind you. It wasn't normal. I have never been a man meant for just one woman, so make of that what you will. My days and nights were filled with her large black eyes and her arousing, animal scent and that laughter. Oh...that sweet, mocking, crystalline laughter that haunted even my dreams. I began to neglect my business. I stopped counting the money that came in, which upon her arrival seemed to increase spectacularly. I ceased to care for my appearance and cleanliness, which as you can see, looking at me right now, was and still is very important to me. At night, when it was time for sleep, I would close my eyes but only dreams would come. Dreams of stroking Adulphina's supple skin, tasting her lips and exploring the black, delicious wonders entombed between her legs.

I know now this woman was no woman at all, and she was not of this earth. Such explains the hold she had over me.

Very soon those sweet dreams and fantasies began to change. Becoming more like nightmares which would not go away even when I was wide awake. My sensual fancies soon became corrupted with mirages and flavors of the profane. In the dreamworld, she began to seem less human. Less real. Her flawless flesh, in a certain patch of shadow, would appear scaly like a crocodile. The eyes too big for her skull, bulging out grotesquely like explosions of fungus erupting from the stump of a dead tree. A queer odor would sometimes follow her, a reek reminding me of damp things and empty rooms. Lonely smells reserved for churches and affairs of the grave. Then it would all be gone, as if she had snapped her fingers and wished it away. Even now, knowing what I do, I wonder if it really ever happened. I must remind myself again and again, especially at night when the room is dark and quiet and I am trapped with my thoughts, that it did happen. It *did* happen, amigo.

On Saturday nights Adulphina would come out and perform a musical number on our stage. More of a striptease with a bit of singing, really. She would croon out in her low, husky purr of a voice. Singing in a tongue strange to me. But it did not matter what she was saying in these songs. It was the way she would sing, you see. The manner in which she swayed her hips, whipped her long dark hair, and shook her gorgeous ass. She could have been singing a litany for the dead and everyone would feel compelled to listen, stopping in their tracks to watch her the way a mad dog is mesmerized into submission with the sob of a violin.

With her came a pianist, a drummer and a saxophone player, three cadaverous men whom I had never met, never learned their names or where they had come from. Nor did I want to. Like her, the three of them seemed to have walked through a door from another world, a world where the dead and the living walked very close, side by side. Their performance would inevitably send our patrons into a wanton frenzy. By the end of their show, which felt much more like a ritual, every living thing on the dance floor, even any police present, would find themselves naked and sweating and moaning and performing perverse acts with others they would never dream of doing beyond the walls of the Starlight. Things which made even an old reprobate like myself blush like a virgin bride. I would always excuse myself from these festivities when they would begin to devolve into chaos, retiring to my table reserved in the back with my hookah and enough spiced hashish to distract my attention from the display of reckless sensuality unfolding upon the dance floor. It was as if I were utterly impotent in my ability to stop what was happening.

I didn't mind the Saturnalia, to be honest. I have always been a brazen hedonist, and I find absolutely nothing wrong with humoring oneself with whatever pleasures of the flesh one wishes to discover so long as everyone involved is of a proper age to agree to the diversions being explored. But things didn't stay that way. The pesky concepts of *normalcy* and *decency* were things that didn't exist at Club Starlight after Adulphina had come to take over as mistress of ceremonies.

Soon I began to see things I did not want to see. Dreadful, brutal, and unholy activities. I swear to you my rotund friend, upon the sainted life and memory of my sweet mother, Carmelita Maria Justina Grau, I know these were not illusions or brain fevers. Before my shocked eyes I would see caresses and kisses relent to feats of bloodshed and sadism. Knives would appear in hands and shimmer in the strobing lights of the overhead dance floor rig, slicing through skin and drawing forth gouts of blood. Howls of torture and groans of rapture would fill the room, drowning out the rumble and crash of the music. Flesh being peeled away from skulls and bones and chewed and gnawed as I watched, mouth agape, unable to avert my eyes. People, no longer acting human, gorging themselves upon the meat and juices of their fellow sinners. Even the corpses of those unfortunate enough to have been singled out for butchery by the mob were not exempt from carnality and desecration. And all I could do was just sink into the cushions of my booth and watch, helplessly. Smoking my hashish, enraptured, aroused, and nauseated. Through it all her low, sultry whispering in my head to come to her. Come to her and join them in their fiendish sacrament.

Inevitably I would pass out, and upon awakening I would find myself in my bed, tucked in snug as you like, not recalling how I had got there. The previous night's debauchery was a faint, but definite, disagreeable aftertaste lingering in my brain. That is what rendered me powerless for so long, that incapacity to affirm that all of this lunacy was just the dreaming of a sick man addled on too much gin and hashish. But very soon, thankfully, all of this would come to an end. When others began showing up at the club asking questions.

During the winter of that final year, when my sanity was truly circling the drain, people began coming to the club in the hours before we opened. People asking about things I could not answer. Wives and husbands and sisters and mothers and friends, all of them looking for people in their lives who had come to the Starlight but never returned to their homes. Some brought photographs with them. A few threatened to contact the authorities, a joke in and of itself. Little did they know *[chuckles]*. Instead of directing these poor souls to me, the owner, the staff had been instructed to show them to Adulphina's office, a chamber I had built on to the structure just for her and in which I had never even set a single toe.

After speaking with her, they would leave the club as if in a trance. Bewitched. Their eyes wide and glassy and dazed. Rarely would these people return. But every so often, Adulphina's sorcery wouldn't completely take hold of one person here and there. They would sometimes return to the club in the evening hours and make an awful scene. Mordo, the tall, skeletal goon the witch had hired as her personal servant, would grab that poor soul by the shirt collar or sometimes even by the hair of their head and drag them howling and kicking from the premises, out into the shadowy streets and nooks of Lisbon, never to be seen or heard from again.

This too began to weigh heavily upon me. How many people had vanished from the world because of what I had done? What had I created? And I *am* to blame. With this there is no room for argument. But I was powerless. Adulphina was in control, and there was no way I could snatch this power back away from her. I was too old. Too weak. I had let it go on for too long.

(A pause. The sounds of muffled voices and the clinking of what might be ice cubes rolling around in a glass tumbler. This goes on for well over a minute before the narration resumes)

Then came that evening in June. The day of the summer solstice. A night so hot people still talk about it to this day. This was the day when I would finally find my freedom from the Starlight Club.

The night had started off as normal as could be expected for my little pocket of perversion. People were dancing, and drinking, and laughing. A pretty low key evening, to be honest. Adulphina sat in her chair, a throne, really, in the little balcony alcove I had built so she could gaze down on to the dance floor like a giant queen wasp surveying her crawling, mindless workers, Mordo at her side like always. As usual, I had begun drinking very early. Before we had even opened our doors and the sun was still burning in the clouds. But it seemed no matter how much booze I marinated myself in, I could not get drunk. It was as if something were fighting me. Something within myself, forcing me to remain clearheaded and aware. I know now it was a warning, an advisement to keep my wits about me. A message from some kindly spirit who had perhaps taken pity upon an ancient degenerate.

As the night wore on, the festivities grew more fevered and intense. No different than usual, really. But there was something slithering about in the air. A creeping unease. Something huge was about to happen. You could actually feel it in the flesh, building and swelling and growing. Like a huge mouth opening up, tongue uncurling, beckoning the unwary. I had stopped drinking and now merely sat watching. The tension in the club was a flexed muscle.

At the stroke of one minute past midnight, now officially the solstice, Adulphina rose from her throne and held up her thin, ghostly hand for silence. There was immediate quiet. Feet stilled on the illuminated dance floor. All eyes were on her. She then began to speak in a language I could not comprehend. Now I know the tongue in which she spoke belonged to the living dead. A secret and sinister dialect known only to the ambassadors of the damned. The words, each and every syllable infused with the charms of Hell, made my head swim. I felt as if I were floating upon a great, raging river, barely hanging onto a child's inflatable beach toy for safety. I stood up and tried to make my way toward the exit, feeling the walls for support, for my eyes had proven unfaithful. The witch's band began to play behind her as she continued her incantation, a deafening racket that all but devoured all other traces of sound.

My eyes were drawn to the dance floor. This was one

of those grand old disco dance floors alive with shifting and flickering patterns of light. The lights sparkled and slithered in time with the beat of the music, splitting and mending themselves into mesmerizing shapes and pulses of electric color, until finally settling into the outline of a definite image. Clear as day, the bulbs under the floor had collected themselves into the shape of the Devil's emblem, the five-pointed star. A pentagram etched in red neon against a black background, shimmering and pulsating. As if calling out to someone.

A man at the bar stood up and began walking toward the floor, stripping away his clothes one article at a time until he stood naked in the center of the pentagram. In one hand he held a kitchen knife. He turned to Adulphina and offered up what I took to be some kind of salute. He wanted her to see what was going to come next. What came next is something that I will never forget.

The man fell to his knees, whispering strange words under his breath, fantastic colors swimming beneath the floor like a swarm of ghostly snakes. I hadn't realized he had cut into himself until I saw the sprawl of dark fluid pool on the floor, spreading slowly out like a flowering magnolia blossom. Not a single peep. Not one hushed gasp of pain. Not even when he held up his dripping, slimy testicles into the light for her approval. A sacrifice of flesh and blood to enter her paradise. But it was more than that. This was more than an offering. I recognized this to be what it truly was: this was a key being inserted into a lock on a door closed for many years. A door leading into another world. The world Adulphina had come from.

I have come to learn in my many travels since leaving Lisbon there are things in this world we do not, and will not, ever understand. What awaits us after death is the greatest mystery of all. I think there are all sorts of things waiting in between all of that, and it is easy for a soul to get lost in those between places when they are looking for the true hereafter.

The poor man, his ruined manhood still clutched in his fist, pitched over onto his face and lay twitching on the dance floor as the pentagram glowed brighter. Within seconds, the crowd was on their feet and falling upon him, like wolves mangling a crippled deer, tearing into his flesh and rending his hide from the bones within seconds. A horrible, gory supper which I could only watch as a disgusted observer.

While the mob fed upon this man's blood and meat, the dance floor began to creak and rumble, a faint crack splitting down the middle of the dance floor glass as the earth beneath the club weakened and gave way to dirt. There was the sound of splintering wood, and from the ruin of black soil and glass a withered, grey hand shot up and grasped at the air, the black nails on its fingertips raking across the floor. Another hand soon joined it, then another. Something pointy and metal emerged. It took me a moment to realize it was the rusted helmet of a Conquistador captain, the bent steel imprisoning a grinning, skeletal horror of a face. Another followed, then two more. The dance floor shattered and collapsed, revealing the burial ground which had been hidden beneath it. The forgotten crypt of the dead Spanish soldiers now stirred back into wakefulness by the lure of their newly awakened, profane lust.

The stench in the room grew utterly unbearable. The sourness of old rot, curdled earth, and the putrescence of evil smothering out the usual odors of beer and cigarettes, of sweat and perfume. I knew I was smelling the arousal of the living dead. It would seem the thirsts and desires of these men, although long dead, had not dissipated in the long centuries since falling to the reaping edge of Death's blade.

What came next was a nightmare made all the more terrible by the fact I *knew* it was real. The shambling, decayed husks of the mighty Portuguese warriors reached out to take carnal comfort from the living. Some piling three ghouls to one living person, not caring if their paramour were man or woman. There was only the need to rut and spoil and profane. The club was humming with the horrible moans and gasps of pleasure and terror flowing perfectly together. Adulphina's dreadful, beautiful laughter ringing in my ears. She was laughing at me. Mocking my repulsion.

Join us, old rooster. Join us in our most dreadful of delights...

I sprang into action, my legs moving as if guided by puppet strings. I tell you right now I felt the presence of the Almighty in my body. As if God himself had entered my bones long enough to clear my head and give my body agency to escape this hell on earth I had unwittingly created. But Adulphina would not be thwarted so easily. I could feel her delicate, soft touch upon my body. Her lips upon mine and her tongue in my mouth. But when I would open my eyes she would still be in her alcove, eyes glowing deep pink with the flames of Hell burning behind them. I knew then that if I didn't get out, if I didn't escape that room right then, I would become a part of it forever. I waded and shoved my passage through the decaying, fetid demons locked in all manner of lewd relations with the living. Focusing on that little voice in my head guiding me, blocking out Adulphina's terrible song, averting my eyes from the perversions lapping at my heels.

Through crimson stained deserts and across windswept, desolate beaches I walked. Through a kingdom carved from shadows, stuck between two worlds. My shoes were full of cold, wet sand and my clothes were filthy with the slime of the awakened, sinful dead. A cold red sun shone down, my bones shivering from the chill of undeath it radiated upon an abandoned, extinct world. The tips of icy fingers brushed across the back of my heel and the collar of my shirt, desperately trying to grab me and return me to their Queen. Back to Adulphina, back to the wreck of my life.

Do not return, old rooster. A word of warning for an old friend. *You have no place here any longer.*

And she was right. I might have built that cursed nightclub, but it was her place. Her church, where only the utterly faithful were permitted to linger.

I am not sure how I did it, but I made it out of the club. The last thing I remember was being outside the Starlight and it looking very different to me. What I saw only served to corroborate the macabre affairs of the past months. Attesting to the afflicted disposition of the land. The club, from the outside, looked as if it had not been open for many months, perhaps even years. The windows were boarded up and smudged with dust and fly shit, the asphalt of the parking lot cracked and neglected, devilgrass and briar busting out of the ground and through the rock. Behind the windows there was only a deep, dark desolation. No more of the witch's song in my skull. No more bray of a haunted saxophone, tinkling of warped piano keys, or plucking of a dead man's guitar. Groans of ecstasy and suffering gone silent. A couple of rats scurried out of a drainpipe and into the nearby canal and all around me the sounds of the city. The familiar, comfortable sounds of Lisbon. Traffic and the braying of horns from the boats navigating the waters of the Tejo. The noise of the living.

Behind those dirty windows with their boards and nails and cobwebs, I could still feel them. Feel *her.* They would always be there, until the crack of doom.

I walked half a mile to the nearest payphone and called a taxi to take me to the airport. Once there, I bought myself a one-way ticket to Texas, my choice of destination based upon having watched a John Wayne movie about the Alamo the night before, and I have not returned to the shores of my homeland ever since. Nor do I plan to. I understand completely that I am no longer welcome there, and to go back would be to court my undoing. Even if the Starlight is no longer standing, I know Adulphina is still hanging around, somewhere, working her evil from the shadows of her alcove for a last call that never ends. I am the one who conjured her, and I know in my darkest of hearts that she will never leave. That the Devil will always have one eye open and a song upon her lips, just for me. Waiting. Hungry. Mark my words—

The recording ends abruptly, a loud blast of electronic hiss swallowing the old man's voice, the remainder of his story surrendered to static. The folded-up sheet of notebook paper reveals two names and a strange series of numbers.

Lina – 286 Rua Do Vale
Soledad – 117 Calcada de Santana

If there are two more tapes to follow, as indicated by the markings on the original cassette, they have yet to be found.

5 DELETED SCENES FROM VAMPIRO LAMIA

Gwendolyn Kiste

Alternate Opening Sequence

You're alone in the theater when the first shot of the movie materializes on the screen. It's a close-up on a pool of blood, thick as maple syrup, brighter than Merlot. You can't make sense of it for a moment. There's no context, only a gentle *drip-drip-drip* down a marble staircase.

Then the camera pulls back, and you see her. The vampire priestess, her dark hair flowing down her shoulders, her winged eyeliner in the shape of a cat's eye. There's a stain on one side of her mouth and a strange glint in her eye.

And right on cue, the title flashes over the screen, written in—what else?—jagged, red letters.

VAMPIRO LAMIA

You smile a little because you know everything about this movie. How it had a limited first run in theaters, back in '71 or '72, more than half a century ago now, more than a decade before you were even born. But somehow, it doesn't feel that long ago. It feels like this story is still happening, that it never stopped happening, and that it never will.

The names are scrolling by the screen now, and you've got them all memorized. Starring Marisol Lucas as the vampire priestess who must contend with angry villagers as well as an amateur gumshoe determined to smoke out the bloodsucking cult and destroy them once and for all. Written and directed by husband-and-wife team David and Theo Jackson, who were collaborators on a string of low-budget pictures, each one bloodier than the last, all of them featuring Marisol Lucas in a leading role.

Vampiro Lamia was the culmination of this unholy cinematic alliance, the final hurrah of the series. It isn't their best film, not by a mile, but it's still probably your personal favorite. A guilty pleasure.

The discordant score is blaring through the speakers, the synthesizer and fretless bass playing over a grisly montage, the cuts rapid-fire. In intricate close-ups, a man's throat is ripped open and another man's after that and another and another until it's a psychedelic abattoir, the screen becoming the bloodiest tie-dye you've ever seen.

All the while, the beautiful, beaming vampire feeds.

Marisol Lucas feeds.

You sit back, your head dizzy. There's something every fan of the movie remembers about Marisol. How she died in a fiery car crash at the age of thirty-six, still in her prime, still making horror movies right up to the very end. In fact, she was headed to the set of the Jacksons' latest film for the first day of shooting when it happened. A Dead Man's Curve, a dead girl's bad luck. There were no next of kin, no one except her co-stars to bury her body. She lived her life in the cinema and nowhere else, appearing suddenly in these strange films, only to vanish into the mist just as quickly.

But for now, you try not to think about any of that. Instead, you focus on her face, on the way the bloodied corners of her lips twitch upwards, the opening music coming to a manic crescendo.

And as the shot fades to black, all she can do is close her eyes and smile.

The Vampire Priestess Meets Her Match

There's a jump cut in the footage, and all at once, there she is again, arrayed in a flowing blue dress. Marisol as the vampire priestess is showing a new guest around the castle, revealing hidden corridors and passageways within the dusty stone walls.

"This is where you belong now," the vampire tells the girl, who secretly fancies herself a supernatural sleuth. She's the granddaughter of a villager who was found in a mass grave, his body drained and broken. Now she's here to avenge his death, to avenge all the dead villagers who came before him. But the vampire is intimately aware of her plan. In fact, they each know the other one's intentions. They can't both survive this intact.

When they reach the highest tower of the ancient castle, the two of them chitchat for a moment in the moonlight, the dialogue dubbed slightly out of sync, giving everything a jarring, surreal quality that makes you feel out of place, out of time.

You can understand why they cut this scene. It's overlong and plodding, just an elaborate establishing shot, and let's face it: you don't need it. After all, each of these old vampire films required at least one sprawling estate. Where else are you going to hide the ever-growing mound of bodies?

But if you're being honest with yourself, you can understand exactly how a vampire priestess like her could lure so many to their deaths. Even now, decades after her own brutal end, Marisol Lucas is irresistible, all shining potential, her pale eyes gazing out at you from the screen, seeing everything and nothing.

For the first time, you glance around the theater. You're still all alone, which is exactly how you like it. But there's something else, something that's starting to gnaw at you. You don't quite remember how you got here. This must be one of those limited engagement screenings, the kind where just a select few fans get to see the excised sections of a cult classic. But you don't remember any invitation. You don't remember buying a ticket or sashaying past the concession stand or even picking the very seat you're sitting in. It's as if you were coaxed from the void to be a wide-eyed spectator for the movie. Like maybe the movie needs you to see its broken pieces, these scenes that were cut out of it like a desperate, beating heart.

"I'm here," you whisper, and you nearly laugh aloud at yourself. There's no one around, which means there's no one listening.

So you return to what you do best. You stare up at the screen and absorb the film. Meanwhile, the film is absorbing you, drawing you closer, draining you, bit by bit, the same way Marisol does to her victims, always making you feel like you're a part of it.

Isn't that what all the greatest movies do?

A Vampire's Forgotten Tragedy

On the screen, the light changes, shifting from a cool yellow to a bright sea blue, and you blink back in the saturated glow. The edges of the frame shimmer, and you realize it in an instant: you're in a flashback now, hopscotching decades into the past, into where this all started. The vampire priestess and the amateur gumshoe are arrayed in long, tight dresses and leather waist cinchers, the kind you might see at a Renaissance Faire. It seems odd that someone would want to remove this footage, considering the rest of the film hardly makes sense without it.

You watch, breathless, as the vampire priestess, a mere mortal then, leans in, her lips brushing against the cheek of the gorgeous detective who's no more than a wistful maiden. The two of them were lovers once, many centuries ago, back when it was forbidden to be who they were, to love who they loved.

They did their best to keep it quiet, but as always, the villagers found out about them, about the way they held each other in the night, and they did what villagers in horror movies do best. They destroyed everything. They used fire. They used ropes. They even used their bare hands. And when they were done, there were no girls left to speak of.

Your heart tightens in your chest, because it isn't fair. The world shouldn't keep two people apart, not for any reason, but especially not for that reason.

For what it's worth at least, the vampire priestess makes the world pay. She rose from her shallow grave, revenge boiling in the impossible depths of her cold heart. Somehow, though, the price of blood doesn't seem a steep enough penalty for what those villagers did, but it will suffice just the same.

You creep forward in your seat, relishing every moment of bitter revenge. She shows them just how to use fire to its best effect. She shows them how to use ropes and hands and teeth, too. The bodies pile up like autumn leaves, and as yet another villager gets his jugular ripped out, the vampire's gleeful mouth smeared red, you let out a whoop that ricochets off the ceiling.

You can't quite recall if you've always cheered her on. That's because you barely remember seeing this film for the first time. You must have been in college then, sitting cross-legged on a futon in a group of bleary-eyed coeds, the room completely dark except for the halo of the screen. A clumsy grad student had his hand up your blouse, his tongue repeatedly wetting his lips, but you mostly ignored him. In that moment, all you cared about was the movie.

And in this moment, all you still care about is this footage, these forgotten scenes that should never have been lost to time. Right now, it feels like the only thing in the world that really matters. Like the only thing that's ever mattered.

The Vampire Priestess and Her Glorious Cult

By now, the audience knows her. They know how the vampire priestess tore out the throats of many men, their bodies picked clean, their bones blanching in the moat around the castle. But that doesn't mean she was without mercy. Over the decades, she occasionally spared an occasional beautiful woman or two. If by *spare*, you mean the way she transformed them into her undead companions, while she waited for her true love to rise from the ashes and join her at last.

They've gathered in the ballroom now, all the women blood-crazed ghouls, their hands curled into claws, their eyes gone blacker than a Yuletide midnight.

"Don't stop, my lovelies," the vampire priestess whispers, and together, they surround a sneering band of men who crept into the castle, determined to destroy them. The men realize too late who's really going to be destroyed.

The scene lasts nearly five minutes, and it's a bacchanalia of bloodletting, splashes of gore splattering on the walls, on the floor, even on the camera lens itself. To be honest, you can see why this didn't make the final cut. It might have been a bit superfluous, considering the rest of the film had more than its fair share of cult rituals and marvelous mass murders, the death count rivaling any slasher film of later eras.

But maybe this sequence is more than that. Maybe it's an opportunity to see all these women together, frolicking and fearsome, afraid of nothing and no one. Maybe it's the chance to witness them in all their glory. They hold hands as they finish off the wayward men, taking turns with their bodies, one after another, the girls like a gruesome daisy chain.

Meanwhile, Marisol as the vampire priestess looms over it all, looking more alive than anyone you've ever seen. It doesn't seem real that she could be gone from the world, not when she's right there, not when she's ruling a fierce kingdom all her own.

You recline in your seat, soaking in the slaughter, the cool shadows of the theater feeling like all you'll ever need.

Except that's not entirely true—there is something else you need.

As the villa of vampires parades across the screen, their bodies bathed in gore, you want to know what it feels like in their embrace. With their hunger never sated, you want to know what it's like to be devoured whole.

And when they're done with you, their mouths stained and eager, you want to become just like them.

Alternate Ending

You've seen this film dozens of times, which means you

already know how it turns out for the vampire priestess.

(Spoiler alert: not well.)

She's waited all these years for her lover to return, to reincarnate in present day, only for that same woman to bury a stake dead-center in her heart. In the theatrical run—and all the bootlegs that followed—you always cringed during those last two minutes, at the series of muddy shots and quick cuts.

The grand hall of the castle.

Footsteps and a flash of a shadow.

A splintered piece of wood.

The discordant music from the opening shot, come back to haunt our lovely, lonely vampire.

She doesn't beg for her life. She only reaches out for her lover who refuses to reach back. The sun rises behind them, and the stake comes at her all at once. A strangled gasp. A mound of ash. Then it's done, a crude *The End* plastered on the screen before the last reel spins out.

It's the one part of the film you never could stomach. The one part that you couldn't quite fathom.

That's because it's not the way it really ended. The original cut was entirely different. Marisol and the two directors fought for their finale, fought until the bitter end, but it did no good. Studios always get what they want, whether they deserve it or not. They're like the villagers in that way. Destructive and cruel and not knowing what's good for them. Or what's good for anyone else, either.

And now at last, you get to see the real thing. The proper denouement, how *Vampiro Lamia* was always meant to finish.

The vampire priestess is in the highest tower of the castle again. The unmotivated red lighting casts sharp shadows across her cream complexion, and the amateur detective—her reincarnated lover—is with her now.

"Shall you finish me for good and all?" the vampire priestess asks, but this time, her lover's hands shake, agony in her eyes, and she can't go through with it. She collapses into the monster's arms instead. Into the arms of the woman who worships her.

This is how it was meant to be, the way you always wanted it to end. The way you want it to end for *you*.

And maybe you'll get your wish. There are whispers all around you, and there's giggling too, and you don't even have to look around to realize it: you're not alone in the theater anymore.

Perhaps you were the only one invited here for a reason. Perhaps being the film's biggest fan has advantages you never dreamed of.

The final deleted scene is still playing on the screen in front of you, but you don't need to watch it anymore. You already know how this all ends. The vampire priestess and her lover are together in the last frame, their bodies wrapped up with one another, their satin dresses soaked red with blood. In this singular moment, Marisol gets her happy ending. She gets to endure for all eternity.

Their murmurs are growing louder, and you can sense them all around you, their long flowing dresses and their mouths desperate for a taste.

"This is where you belong now," the cult whispers, their voices echoing as one, their figures hungry and harried and lovelier than you could ever imagine.

And as they lean in toward you, their teeth sharp and ready, all you can do is close your eyes and smile while the final frame of the film fades to glorious black.

THE COUNTESS OF CRUELTY

Sam Richard

Asa,

I'm honestly not sure why I'm writing. My psychiatrist said it would be a good idea, that maybe I could get some closure out of it, but I think he's full of shit. Closure? Are you fucking kidding me? How could I ever find closure? I think he's a goddamn hack. But I can hear your voice in my head telling me to give it a try anyhow. Reassuring me that if it might help, I should do it regardless of how I feel right now.

And you called me the stubborn one.

Fuck. I miss you so much. Nothing's the same without you. Life isn't worth living. Nothing has color anymore. You would have loved the funeral, I mean, well, you know...

Your mom picked out the flowers. They were perfect. And a ton of people came, so that's something at least. If I'm being honest, I don't remember half of it. Just a sea of blurry faces and arms hugging me while I repeatedly broke down in tears until there was nothing left. It would have been so much easier if you had been there, which I guess is the ultimate irony, huh?

I'm going away for a while. Figured it was time to finally travel outside of the USA. Scotland, just like we always talked about. God, why can't you be here? I hope it helps me clear my head, maybe get some new perspective, though I say that and new perspective is all I've had recently, so I guess I'm just looking for an escape for a while. The house is so fucking empty without you. Everything is so empty without you.

The words of a letter, taken at random from a shoebox atop a crumbling box of old books, bore into Frank. Surrounded by the dusty remnants of another's life, pulled into a stranger's forgotten and abandoned trauma and grief... It's too much.

The earth shakes, pulling him to the floor in tears. Through the haze, it registers how filthy the attic truly is, but the thought swims in that sea of observations he's coherent enough to have, but that's not coherent enough to rise above. It's just grief now. Another daily reminder that she's gone. Another moment of pure fucking panic. Inescapable.

Until I'm dead, too.

The letter rips Frank in pieces. His tears splash against the brittle yellow paper of the envelope. The worst waves of grief always come out of nowhere. Just an ordinary Tuesday spent cleaning the attic of his new house, sorting through the remnants of lives spent here before. You never anticipate the ice in your veins, and it hits at random. It's crippling.

Dust dances around him as he cries, kneeling on the

ragged wooden floor of the unfinished room. Just like a thousand other days in a thousand other places. Spiders fidget in the shadows, haphazard stacks of boxes litter the large open room. But this is as far as he gets, grabbing the shoebox full of letters, Frank walks down the questionable ladder, closes it up behind, and heads to the dining room table. Emily's dining room table. One she got from her parents when she moved out at 18. Worn and chipped, but beautiful.

The rest of the house is barely unpacked from the move. An exodus from Minneapolis to small town Wisconsin. Stacks of boxes and upended furniture litter most of the rooms.

The worn envelopes rub strangely against his skin. He breathes heavily, smelling the musty odor of decades of storage. Abandoned, discarded.

It worms into him. Not just the grief of the letters, but what they mean, and what it means that they've since been forgotten. Memories only he and Emily shared, now carried by one. Stories she told him that she may have never told anyone else. The surviving memorial of their life. Of her life.

And now these letters. Someone else's private, deeply personal pain and grief. A burden as much as an honor.

He flips one letter back in the pile, hoping they're in order, and opens it with delicate care.

Asa,

Well, I did it, I'm in Scotland. Glasgow, to be exact. Gonna head up to the tip of the Highlands soon though, hopefully catch a ferry onto an Orkney Island or two...

Is it weird that I haven't written you in a while? Probably weirder that I'm acting like you could respond, or that you'll ever read these. Your family all miss you so goddamn much. Your dad cried when I left, and you know more than anyone how unlike him that is. He bought my plane ticket, too. Said he'd have been happy to do it for us both if you were still here. Thought it would be good for me to get out of the house, out of the city, out of grief, I suppose.

I told your mom I was writing you. She said it sounded like a good idea and maybe she would, too. So expect to 'hear' from her, I guess. Fuck.

Why, Asa? Why are you fucking dead. Fuck. Fuck. Fuck Fuck. I love you more than I could ever express when you were still alive and, honestly, I'm afraid this will destroy me. I'm sure it will. Fuck, now I'm crying again.

I'm gonna go. I'm so sorry you aren't here. I'm so fucking sorry you died.

My Eternal Love,
Suzie

It's too familiar. The loss, anger, bafflement, utter *what-the-fuck* of it all fit like a glove. His tears run dry; a numbing cloud fills his chest. Emily should be here. To find these letters. She would have held them close to her heart, she would have honored them in a way few others could.

But how different would that have been? A normal afternoon discovery. Condensation-covered beers and 80s post-punk while they cleaned. The joy of first-time homeownership. A break taken from the dust and grime of the attic, spent devouring a box of old letters addressed to a ghost.

A perfect afternoon.

Instead, it's too real. Too personal. Too parallel. It's all so strangely wrong given that he shares the burden, that he's on a similar path. No chance to separate. No distance.

Asa,

This castle is fucking amazing. Ok...*castle* might be a strong word. Manor? Fuck, I don't know. Mansion? It doesn't matter. What matters is how goddamn cool it is. I spent the afternoon wandering the halls, trying to take in the whole place. The floors are lined with dark red carpeting with filigree patterns and elegant detailing. There's antique furniture everywhere and the bed has this ornate canopy with bed posts that damn near hit the ceiling.

You would love it...

There's...there's this painting, though.

This painting that looks just like you.

It's fucking haunting. Creeps me out every time I see it. It also makes me long for you. You, or the woman in the painting, are standing on some rocks at the edge of a garden. There are dark, foreboding clouds gathering behind you/her. Her.

Her.

She's holding onto the leashes of two giant Doberman Pinschers. Her eyes are a terrifying kind of empty. They're so black. Abysses I could fall into. I've never seen anything like it before. Not just the uncanny resemblance, but the emotions the painting gives off. It's honestly terrible. I dread walking down the hall it's in, but I have to, to get to my room, even though I want to see her because she's you.

It makes me miss you all the more. You would look at it and laugh, reassuring me that there's nothing to be afraid of. But you don't understand, Asa. The woman's eyes. I see them in the darkness. I see them in my mind. She watches me from her garden perch even when I'm not at the manor. She watches me without seeing me. It freaks me out.

And I know this is probably all just a manifestation of my grief. *Trauma-induced paranoia* or something of the sort. I'm sure my therapist would have a term for it. But it feels so real.

And you're so fucking far away now.

I'm afraid her image will replace yours in my mind when I think of you. That she'll crawl in there and root around, changing memories, distorting how I feel.

When I write these letters, I feel crazy.

I'm sorry you're not here. Why aren't you here?

I'm sorry you're dead. Why are you dead?

Love,
Suzie

A chill crawls through Frank. Equal parts confusion, compassion, and a strange sense of fear all meet in the middle of his chest. He knows how easy it is to let grief consume you. To lose your footing. He gently folds up the letter and places it back in its envelope.

A hot shower washes off the dust of the attic, but isn't

abrasive enough to scrub either the lingering eerie sensation, nor the raw nerve of sorrow dredged up by the letters. Drying off and hopping into bed, he hopes for the stillness of night to lull him into rest.

Silken hair against his back wakes him. Soft breathing on the other side of the mattress. A dreamlike comfort of not being alone, but laced with vague fear. The thing shifts and gently moans. He imagines hot breath on Emily's pillow for the first time since she died. He imagines this thing beside him forming like dense liquid to fill the shadow burned into the spot she left behind.

Tears trickle from his eyes and across the bridge of his nose. The thing pressing against him breathing in and out and in and out. It sounds just like her. The darkness pulls him back, wrapping his sorrow in a shroud of nothing.

Morning light cascading on the far wall wakes him and he shakes free from the night's grief. He rubs the harsh sleep from his eyes as he makes a cup of coffee with a splash of bourbon. The heat of the mug irritates his palm and finger, but he kind of likes it. It reminds him that he is alive. Sitting at the table, he opens another letter.

Asa,

This place is officially fucked. I want to leave but being on an island, I don't exactly get to decide when. Next ferry isn't for three more days. I hear something out in the halls at night. Some *thing* prowling the dark corridors. Maybe more than one. Claws clattering against the wooden floors. Heavy breathing. Howls echoing across the castle.

Something presses against the walls and my door at night.

I think I'm losing it.

But I also feel you here with me. Last night you came to me in a dream. But your eyes were off. Empty holes. Almost soulless. I was so excited to see you. We embraced and spoke, but I couldn't look into the pits where your eyes should be. And your voice was so strange and hollow. But it was you. I cried. You held me. We fell into each other and I got lost. There was nothing but you and I in this endless swirl of skin and hair and tongues and mouths and fingers and sweat and we opened into each other. It was beautiful. But it hurts.

It hurts so fucking much.

And when I looked at you after, for one brief moment, you weren't you. You were someone else. Someone repulsive and vile and I panicked and ran.

I woke up with the door open and mud on the other side of the bed.

And these beasts still roam the halls.

Why can't you be here? Why are you dead and now I'm alone for fucking ever and surrounded by such madness and I can't leave...

Why.

Why.

Why.

He knows the sensation of being pulled into madness. Something tickles the back of his neck as he remembers the dream of the woman in his bed. Not the same, but not much different.

But that isn't new. So many dreams and nightmares since she died. So many instances of waking up crushed that she isn't in bed next to him like he'd been imagining in his sleep. The nightmare being the harsh truth of reality and the dream going unanswered.

If only she were still alive...

It doesn't work that way, though, and it will drive you insane if you let it. First the longing, then the anger, which swells up into bitterness, and that brings the internalized rejection of other people and their happiness, and it goes deeper and worse until you're a husk of a human being. He knows he doesn't want that. He already watched that happen with his father, who never got over the death of his wife. And they had forty-eight years together. Not a mere nine.

I should be the bitter one...

But it's always a trap. There's nothing good on the other end of that thought. Just poison and more pain. Perhaps a different pain, but one that festers and eats away at you. One that clogs all reasoning and empathy and love. It's impossible to grow or learn or adapt in that state. There is only greater suffering.

Frank gets up to get some water, just something to break up the noise in his mind. He crosses the threshold to the kitchen and is no longer in his house. The walls are adorned with draperies, the floor covered in long rugs spanning the length of a hallway he's never seen or been in. A lingering damp odor fills his nostrils. A painting of a woman who looks just like Emily hangs on the far wall. Something's wrong with her eyes.

A heavy wooden door to his left is cracked open. Inside, someone is screaming, crying, begging. He tries to help them, to rush in and save them, but then he's standing in front of his sink. The tapestries, the rugs, that painting, the door, the ornate molding, the smell of damp are all gone.

Nothing but home.

Shaking his head, the moment passes in a haze. The memory strange and distorted, fading as seconds pass. He fills up a glass and drinks down the water in one gulp before filling it again.

Back at the table, he opens another letter, shaking off the remnants of a moment he can't quite recall. His heart pounds in his chest.

Why?

Asa,

I'm beyond scared. I've heard the dogs roaming the halls, always slightly out of view. Their shadows crawl along the walls day and night and I don't know what's real and what isn't anymore. The caretaker hasn't been back in what feels like weeks, but it can't be that long, can it?

I can't leave. The ferry never seems to arrive and when I leave the manor people stare through me like I'm not even here. I have nowhere to go, no one to turn to. And you're not fucking here. Or anywhere, anymore...

Yet you come to me at night. In fitful

dreams and waking nightmares. Your hollow eye sockets staring back at me. Your unnaturally long fingers pleasuring and torturing me in ways where I no longer know the difference. Feels like this is how it always was. How it always will be...

You held me as I cried last night. It was like being back home, like it was just us on the couch after an especially hard day at work or an evening of stressful social interaction. But it wasn't that. You held me as I cried. Your long hair cascaded over my face, soaking up my tears. Your heavy breathing and rancid breath in sync with the rhythm of my sobbing.

You were taking something from me. Something deep and upsetting.

But now that's all I can remember. You taking from me. You hovering over me. You staring into my soul with your empty eyes and the whining of strange dogs not far in the dark recesses of this crumbing manor, or our crumbling house, or the apartment you had when we first met. Where I moved in with you because I had nowhere else to go and you were so understanding and loving and accepting.

And yet, now all I can see are those abyssal eyes. That cold touch on my skin.

Colder and colder. Like my heart can't beat hard enough to warm up my core.

I'm afraid you're killing me.

The dining room isn't the dining room anymore. It's not like before—that itch of a memory of a sensation. He's in a forest. It's dark, but for the crackle and light of a pitiful campfire he can see through the trees where he's sitting. Standing? Standing.

Frank moves past the trees and into the dull light. On the other edge of the small clearing, just barely within the soft glow of the fire, a group of figures stands, unmoving.

Frank holds his breath, waiting for them to notice him, but they don't. They just stand in the woods, silently, still, but for the fabrics of their clothes gently swaying in the breeze.

Maybe some kind of scarecrow? Art installation?

He moves toward them silently and they remain undisturbed. The smell hits before his eyes can see in the darkness.

Bodies. Six of them, nailed to small crucifixes, some standard, some inverted, some just an X, their frames contorted to match their suffering. Old rot stings his nose, but something beyond that, beyond the death and cruelty hits at his senses, an itch on the back of his brain. There's something worse than wrong.

They're children. All of them. Toddler to teenager. Murdered and put out like Halloween decorations.

He turns away, the weight of their deaths too much for him to take in. Now facing another fire off in the distance, once again in the middle of a cluster of trees. He sprints to it, hoping for something to end the horrors, but unsure of what to do, just fight or flight or faun or freeze, and flight won out.

The next fire is similarly dim, like they were started hours ago, built up, and abandoned.

And barely within the circle of trees, scarcely visible in the low light, another cluster of children. All nailed to crosses. All dead and rotten. But this time, a sign above them:

A Message to the Missionaries

The gallop of feet pounding on dense mud fills the forest, echoing from the darkness. Frank squints, trying to get a read on where it's coming from. Then the growling and barking of dogs. Unnaturally loud. Brutal and vicious.

Too close to react.

Fanged jaws lock onto his arm and neck, pulling him to the mud, squeezing so hard bones crack. A wet gurgle escapes his mouth. The light grows dimmer.

A woman appears from within the trees, beautiful. For a moment, Frank thinks it's Emily. Finally come to meet him at his death, to usher him into the next life where they can be together. She looks down at him with contempt. She's terrifying. They lock eyes as she bends down to him, sickle in hand.

Then screaming. A group of men breaks into the cluster of trees, some with torches, others weapons. A man in the front carrying a large wooden cross yells at her in a thick accent, his words lost to the chaos. The dogs attack, pulling one man to the ground and tearing out his throat.

Several of the men retaliate with axes and large hammers. Frank tries to look away, but he's frozen, his body detached and numb. The splatter of metal against flesh fills the air for a moment, before being drowned out by whimpering and crying of the beasts.

Then the group set their sights on the woman.

Emily?

Her sickle cuts through the air before landing in the neck of one of the men. But it's no use. As he falls, the rest pin her down, all parties screaming; the man with the cross in prayer, the woman in rage, the cluster of men in chaos and violence and revenge.

One towers over her, pulling some tools from his satchel. Two narrow, pear shaped devices with keys on the far end. In the struggle, he smashes them into her face several times before gouging them into her eyes. Dense grey and pink fluid pour out either side of the metal.

Once both are in place, he turns the keys, a little at a time. Her wailing and shrieking is matched only by the eventual cracking of bone which echoes through the trees.

Her screaming continues long after it should, and the squeak of the turning keys meets her in an off kilter-cadence that's eerily musical. Eventually, her orbital bones crack far enough to go quiet, but for the subtle, wet sound of tearing flesh. But her anguished howls continue.

The lights dim again, and Frank floats away into himself, tears streaming down his cold cheeks.

Asa,

I'm so glad that you're back and we can be together again soon. It hurt so much that you and I were a world apart. Thank you for embracing me and telling me that everything will be fine. These fleeting moments of seeing you at night have been wonderful and I'm overjoyed that we can truly be as one, forever.

All the sacrifices you've had to make, I can make them, too. Whatever it is that you need from me, it's yours. No questions asked. I know you hate asking for things. I know you hate needing anything from me. But I will give up anything and everything for you. To you.

And when we are together again, I'll know it was all worth it.

Everything feels so strange now, so I'm going to go, but I'll see you again. And then forever.

In the dining room, with another letter in his hands. But it's not his dining room. A damp chill crawls through him. He's on a chair, surrounded by bare stone walls and wooden barrels.

The letter is different from the others. Red stains cascade across the bottom of the paper and streak up the sides with the occasional thumbprint. Dry. The faraway barking of dogs breaks him from his focus. He stands up and heads for the lone door in the room. The wood is slimy and pulsing, almost as if it's alive, or alive with maggots burrowing under the surface. Before he can pull it open, someone on the other side pushes, sending Frank tumbling back into the center of the room.

She walks in and locks eyes with him, a sense of austere authority and control rolling off her, two giant black dogs following, guarding the door.

Emily?

And maybe, yes, it is, but also, no, it isn't. Frank knows that already. He knows, and he doesn't care.

Her eyes are voids. Blacker than black holes, twin pools of abyss that go on forever. It takes his breath away. She saunters toward him and they embrace, her hair tickling his face, soaking up his tears. He knows it's wrong, that it isn't her, but he also knows he hasn't been right in a very long time.

It feels so fucking good to be in her arms again, to feel her breathing against his chest, to let her in and be one with her. It feels so fucking good to give in to how good it feels, to simply not feel so bad, even for a little while. Even in the embrace of a lie.

When the room goes dark, and there's nothing more

than the sensation of cold steel boring into his brain and the warmth of her touch, he knows he's made the right choice.

It's so much like being home again.

SEE THE LAKES...AND DIE!

Thomas Breen

The bus edged forward in the late morning traffic, its passengers held prisoner to the slow crush of fellow tourists in rental cars. Pedestrians moved freely on the sidewalks, visiting the shops and breathing fresh air.

James sighed, then forced a pained little smile when Chloe touched his knee.

"We're on holiday," she said. "It's OK to enjoy yourself."

They had spent three days in Dublin, with James feeling increasingly exhausted as he trailed after Chloe to the Guinness Brewery, the Jameson's Distillery, some kind of Viking-themed boat cruise, and—three nights running—Temple Bar, where he endured loud music, expensive beer, and thick crowds of Frenchmen and Italians on stag nights.

James would never admit it, but he was feeling his age. When he first took up with Chloe, his sister had warned him that the seventeen years between them was an insurmountable chasm. In those days, wreathed in the warm steam of the most exciting sex he'd ever had in a relationship, he had dismissed Liz's words, but now he knew she had been right.

"What do you even *talk* about?" Liz had asked, over and over. "What do you have in common?"

How could he tell his sister about the uninhibited carnality Chloe had favored him with almost immediately after their first date? It was different for girls her age. They were nothing like the sour, prudish girls he had known in school; her generation grew up marinated in pornography from the moment a parent thrust a phone into their hands.

"She's much brighter than you give her credit for," he had said, sparing his sister the details. "Just because she hasn't gone to university doesn't mean she's some kind of halfwit. You might want to think about examining your class privilege, Liz." This last remark was met with a stare so withering it was a wonder he hadn't dropped dead on the spot.

But of course, Liz had been right. Chloe wasn't at all interested in the things that James cared about, and was content to let him prattle along in lengthy monologues without interjecting a single thought or opinion. And for as long as his head was turned by her taut, athletic body and she shared her depraved ideas about what should happen in bed between a pair of lovers, he hadn't minded.

Lately, though, he had begun to find her grating and dull, noticing more than ever the way she mispronounced simple words, the tedious provincialism of her views of the world, the utter lack of curiosity she displayed whenever he could persuade her to visit an art gallery or classical music performance. Perhaps worst of all, she had begun talking about the dreaded m-word, and every time it passed her lips James pictured himself a prisoner in an old black and white Hollywood film, staring in terror at the camera as the bars of a cell door slam shut in front of him.

Chloe didn't know it, but this holiday in Ireland was a last hurrah of sorts, a final time for him to enjoy her nubile young body and filthy mind before breaking it off and maybe, God forbid, doing as Liz suggested and "finding someone your own age." He would enjoy Ireland as much as possible, and break the news back in London.

Right now, though, the standstill traffic and the coach driver's grating prattle were combining to make it very difficult indeed to enjoy Ireland. James and Chloe had booked a short half-day trip on one of those ridiculous tourist coaches—Pot O' Gold Tours of Eire, with a giant, grinning leprechaun painted on the side—to Glendalough, about an hour south of Dublin, home to some allegedly splendid monastic ruins and a frequently photographed pair of lakes.

The driver was one of those preposterous professional Irishmen James had already come to expect in tourist spots throughout Dublin: red-faced, grinning, "a line of blarney," they'd probably say, meaning an irritating capacity for constant chatter in a brogue whose intensity had to be staged for the benefit of naive tourists.

"While we wait for this bit of traffic to clear up," the driver had said over the coach's public address system, "I'll give you a wee crash course in Irish history, so you can impress everyone on the rest of your visit with how much you know."

Fine, James had thought, anticipating perhaps a Wikipedia-level tour through St. Patrick, Brian Boru, Vikings, all of that. Instead, the driver had launched into a slanted, one-sided view of much more recent history, seeming to relish the details of supposed massacres perpetrated by the tyrannical English on the poor downtrodden natives.

James flipped through the plastic pages of a three-ring photo binder the driver had passed back for the passengers, gazing not at photographs of romantic castle ruins or rugged Aran Island fishing cottages, but at checkpoints swarming with hard-faced soldiers, buildings bombed to rubble in city centers, men in drab green coats and balaclavas, the bearded faces of hunger strikers, sharp and angular, with staring eyes that spoke of alien, fanatic minds, like tortured saints peering out from

Byzantine mosaics.

Surely there was no point in dwelling on all of this, James thought. Why bring it up at all, in fact? Leave it in the past where it belongs, with the potato famine and whatever else. He passed the binder to the passenger in the seat behind him with a little noise of disapproval.

Chloe was holding something gnarled, hard, and black up to his face.

"James, look!" she squeaked with delight. "It's peat!"

"Ah," James said, warily eyeing what looked like a fossilized hunk of human waste.

"Did you hear what the driver was saying about bog mummies?" Chloe asked.

Surely she had misheard, James thought, but then the driver began talking about an exhibit at the National Museum where patrons could view the bodies of murdered men from the Iron Age that had been preserved in peat bogs.

"It's called *Kingship and Sacrifice*, but I'll be honest, they don't look much like kings to me," the driver said. "They look more like something a dog might cough up."

"Oooh, James—we should go and see the bog mummies when we're back in Dublin," Chloe said.

James smiled uneasily. He couldn't imagine anything he would rather do less.

Did these people really put the mangled bodies of murder victims on display like dinosaur fossils?

"We've certainly heard a lot more about massacres and dead bodies today than you typically get on coach trips back home," he said, feigning enthusiasm while trying to be noncommittal.

Chloe smiled and rubbed his knee.

"When in Rome!" she said, a phrase she had been repeating endlessly since they arrived when, he suspected, she didn't know what else to say.

At last, the coach broke free of the Dublin traffic and rolled south through the Wicklow Mountains, the fields around them rippling with waves of bright yellow gorse and storybook sheep in woolen coats that looked like clouds. Even the driver stopped talking about conflict and reprisal long enough to marvel.

"You're a lucky bunch, we don't get many summer days like this in Ireland," he said, his over-emphasized accent slipping for just a moment.

Chloe squeezed James's hand. "It's like driving through a film," she said. He tried to banish his revulsion at the banality of her remark by imagining what she might be wearing under her tights and thin hooded top—or not wearing, as the case may be.

The coach came to a stop in a car park near a small hotel of a design that would have seemed old-fashioned 50 years ago, and a row of little stalls selling souvenirs and ice cream. Before letting his passengers disembark, the driver stood at the front of the coach between the two rows of seats.

"This bus leaves for Dublin at five sharp," he said, no longer smiling. "Not five minutes after five. Not thirty seconds after five. I've got forty souls aboard today, but at five, if I've got thirty-seven souls aboard, then my thirty-seven friends and I are going back to Dublin and the other three can call a cab from the hotel here. It's about seventy euro, by the way, so make sure you're here...when?"

"Five," the passengers said in something like unison.

"Oh no, that's terrible," the driver said, his smile returning. "Let's try again. Make sure you're back here by *when?*"

"FIVE," came the reply, with Chloe joining in with a gleeful shout, causing James to wince.

The driver had been right about one thing, at least: it was a magnificent early summer day, warm and bright and calling to the people of these cold and rainy islands to run outside and turn their faces toward the welcoming sky.

The passengers moved in little groups under the ruined arch that marked the boundary between the sacred and profane at the entrance of the old monastic property, with James scornfully noting that a few of his fellow tourists—Americans, without a single doubt—first stopped at the ice cream stall. Chloe took his hand and smiled, and in spite of himself he felt his irritation dissipating and something like contentment creeping in.

The first site they encountered was the ruin of a monastic city founded in the 6th century by St. Kevin and then, naturally, plundered and sacked repeatedly over the next 800 years by a succession of invaders. What would an Irish site be without a jolly good massacre or two, or three, or seven?

The ruins—a round tower, the walls of what had once been a cathedral, a strange stone church with a sharply slanted roof and narrow belfry—were surrounded by graves of varying age. As they strolled along dirt paths running between monuments, new tombstones emerged, with flowers laid on top of their graves.

"I can't imagine wanting to be buried in a tourist attraction," James said.

"Oh, I think it's lovely," Chloe said. "Just imagine, surrounded by all this history! You'd never get lonely."

James repressed a sigh and looked over a wire fence to some sheep grazing in the field beyond. A few meters further back was a low stone ruin through which gnarled tufts of vegetation grew. It conveyed a sense of unimaginable age, but something else, too: a disorienting feeling radiating from the curiously black stone of its crumbling walls. James wondered if he was seeing distorted waves of heat rising from them, or if that was his imagination.

"Do you think that is an elf church?" a man asked.

Standing next to him was a man about his age, although in marathon runner's shape, with a backpack slung over his shoulders, a tight pair of shorts, and feet swathed in sandals with athletic socks. A German, then.

"What's an elf church?" Chloe asked.

"Ah! Maybe I'm using the wrong words," the man said. "I am thinking of the Irish legends of the faerie folk. Do you know them?"

"Do you mean leprechauns and so forth?" James asked.

"Yes!" the man said excitedly, and slung his backpack round to withdraw something from it. He handed a battered paperback to James. It was *The Fairy Danger in the British Isles: The Real Story!* by an author with the preposterous name Norm Dimble. The lurid, crude cover showed a black and white photo of a mangled body on a country lane with an indistinct blur in the background circled in red.

"Aren't leprechauns supposed to be, I don't know, friendly and jolly and all that?" James said, handing the book to an excited Chloe.

"The book explains that all of that is propaganda," the German said. "It says the fairies lie in wait to trick people so that they make automobile wrecks and building site accidents and similar catastrophes."

"And what do the fairies do then?" Chloe asked, handing the book back.

"They *eat* the *souls* of the victims!" the German shouted, and Chloe gave an excited yelp in reply.

"Well," James said, already regretting asking this possibly insane man to elaborate on his beliefs, "we'll be certain to avoid elves and building sites while here. Come along, Chloe."

The German smiled and gave a little wave with the book as James and Chloe walked down the hill toward the little footbridge that led to Glendalough's famous lakes.

The trail was well-marked. Groups of tourists walked together, looking at the trees in bloom and a little stream running alongside. Chloe's fingers wrapped around James's and they fell into a relaxed stroll.

James wondered if she would be upset when he broke it off with her. Perhaps she was bored with their relationship as well, he thought. Perhaps this would be much easier than he feared, and they could both be adults about it. Maybe she'd even be mature enough for one last night of sex, he thought, his mind turning to the curves of her body and the way she flipped her hair back and forth whenever she'd—

"James! I asked you which way we should go," she said.

They reached a point where the path diverged, one route going up the side of the mountain they had been walking along, the other remaining level. There was no posted sign or directional arrow indicating which way they should go to see the lakes, and James was irritated again. Surely, it's common sense to put proper signage along the route of a major tourist attraction. There was something irreducibly redolent of the developing world about Ireland.

"Well," he said. "The higher lake is the famous one, and so I suppose we should go higher."

A few other people had the same idea, and for fifteen or twenty minutes they walked a gradually steeper path up the mountain in the same contentment they had felt earlier. Eventually, though, they were alone on the trail, and James wondered if they had chosen the right path.

He walked to the edge of the trail, glimpsing something thin and fast moving through the foliage in the dense brush and trees below. Glints of sunlight flashed like reflections off pieces of metal. Some kind of bushwhacking outdoorsy type, James thought.

With the bus driver's stern *FIVE* in his mind, James

was about to suggest doubling back, when they saw a tall, gaunt figure coming down the trail toward them.

It was a priest, or a vicar, or something (*no; they didn't call them vicars here, did they?*), dressed head-to-toe in black, with the clerical collar's speck of white standing out as the man neared. He was very old, possibly in his 80s, but he moved with an easy, loose-limbed grace. As he neared, James realized the priest wasn't just pale, he was an albino, with piercing eyes and a wild tangle of thick white hair blowing about his narrow skull.

"And what do you seek on this lonely road, my friends?" the priest asked, his face and tone unreadable.

"We're looking for the lake, Mr. Father," Chloe said.

"On top of a mountain?" the priest asked. Chloe wrinkled her nose in embarrassment and James felt his face flush.

"Well, you see, the name of the lake is the 'Higher Lake,' at least that's what we were given to understand, and there's no proper signage at all, which I—"

The priest continued as if he hadn't heard James.

"You won't find a lake on top of this mountain. If you seek the lake you'll have to go back down. But if you continue along as you've been, you might see something else, something much rarer, something that not many can say they've seen."

"What's that?" Chloe asked.

"Splendid views of the valley," the priest said, sweeping a long arm in front of him. "On a clear day, you can see as far as the coast, where the longships came and disgorged the men who burned the churches and fed their swords the blood of monks. Not many come this far, not many at all. Most people stay down in the valley, at the lake."

"Is it far to the top then?" Chloe asked.

"Not far, daughter, not far at all," the priest said, and continued past them. James picked up a faint whiff of soil, and shuddered. How relieved he felt that his parents had never burdened him with the nonsense of church and God.

Chloe's excitement returned, and she practically ran up the rest of the trail, with James struggling to keep up, his gaze remaining locked on her firm, bouncing rump as she skipped ahead.

When they reached the top, they saw the priest had been right. The view was breathtaking. Below them were the lakes, the low hills, and scattered forests, stretching out for miles under the summer sun, and for the first time that day James's constant inner gripes were silenced by the beauty around him.

He took Chloe's hand and pulled her into a long, passionate kiss. Did they have time, he wondered, for a quick, cheeky—

"James, a cave!" Chloe shouted, pulling away from him.

He turned with a sigh. A few paces along the summit was, indeed, the low, rocky entrance to what looked like a cave that opened into the mountain. Chloe skipped to the lip of the cave and looked inside.

"Chloe," James said. "I don't think that's an, erm, public cave. I don't see any signs or anything."

"So? Weren't you saying how they don't have enough signs around here, babe?"

She had a point. It would hardly be surprising if whatever tourism authority was responsible for Glendalough failed to properly mark the cave.

"Come on, James, let's go in. They've got lights and everything. It's got to be open to the public."

Reaching the edge of the cave, James saw she was correct: the faint but unmistakable glow of artificial white light beckoned from a few meters inside, illuminating a pathway between the rocky walls.

"I suppose we could take a short look around. But let's be mindful of the time. I don't particularly relish the idea of spending seventy euro for a taxi."

Chloe arched an eyebrow and took a delicate step

inside. The small, circular white lights along the roof of the cave were welcome, as it wasn't long before they walked far enough inside that the day behind them was closed off by a curtain of darkness, the kind only found in a place that has never been touched by the rays of the sun.

"What do you suppose this was for?" Chloe asked, not sure why she was keeping her voice barely above a whisper.

"A mine, I expect," James said. "Possibly a lead mine, maybe tin?"

Much to James's relief, after a few more minutes of walking, Chloe grew bored.

"I think it's time we headed back," he said.

He turned around in the narrow passageway, bracing himself by placing a hand against the bulging, uneven wall. He had only a few seconds to register that the pale white light that had been guiding their way looped down from the roof as a long tendril and wrapped itself around his wrist.

James screamed, which made Chloe scream in response. More of the tendrils, glowing with soft white light, began to drop from the roof of the cave, twitching and circling around James and Chloe, who thrashed and shouted in alarm.

"James, help!" Chloe screamed, but James was pulled further into the cave by the tendril around his wrist. He stumbled. Something strong and relentless was on the other end of the cable. He lost his footing, falling onto the rocky floor to be dragged deeper.

He cried out in pain. Behind him, Chloe shrieked in frantic terror. Grabbing a loose rock with his untethered hand, James bashed at the glowing thing pulling him down, and it recoiled, releasing its grip.

Staggering to his feet, he ran as fast as he could, not daring to touch the walls but not knowing where he was going, and in darkness. He stumbled and tripped a few times, but eventually found a small opening in the rock wall, beyond which a faint light glinted in the distance.

James held his breath and moved sideways through the narrow opening, his soft body scraping against the rock, trying to banish the thought of becoming stuck between those walls, trapped, hopeless, and alone.

Finally, he emerged into a larger opening and saw ahead of him the unmistakable gleam of sunlight. He staggered toward it, and collided with Chloe, who came stumbling from a passageway to his left.

"Oh God, James!" she called. He helped her up, but she fell again. "My ankle," she cried.

In the dim light, he could see she was badly hurt; the ankle might be broken. There was no way she could walk out of here.

"Don't worry," he said, placing his arm under hers so that she was braced against him. "It's not far now."

As they made slow progress toward the light, the walls around them crumbled. More tendrils snaked out toward them. Their unnatural glow lit up the passageway, revealing something much worse.

Emerging from the floor, the roof, and the crumbling walls were shapes that might have once been human: tall, narrow, and covered with ridged muscle the color of sand that looked like raw, rotting meat. In these bodies were embedded chunks of metal from what could have been armor: a broken breastplate, the tilt of a helmet, strands of chainmail embedded in the bubbling, swirling forms.

Whatever he might tell himself later, James did not hesitate. He grabbed Chloe around the waist and flung her toward the things in the cave, turning and scrambling toward the sunlight as her screams were suddenly cut off. Dozens of gaunt, strong hands pulled at her clothes, hair, and into her flesh, ripping out muscle and bone and organs, marking the cave floor with slicks of blood.

Bursting from the mouth of the cave, he ran down the long mountain trail, past the blossoming trees and the rippling gorse and the storybook sheep, across the narrow footbridge and through the cemetery, past the strange small church and the ruined cathedral and the looming round tower, finally clambering onto the coach to plunge down the central aisle and collapse in the seat Chloe had occupied on the ride from Dublin.

As other passengers gradually boarded the bus and the minutes ticked toward five, James covered his head with his arms, unwilling to look out the windows for fear of seeing those shapes from the cave or more glowing tendrils looped among the trees on the edge of the car park.

Finally, the doors whooshed closed and the bus driver walked down the aisle, counting the passengers with his fingers and moving his mouth as the numbers climbed to match the tally on his list.

James curled up in Chloe's seat like a child hiding from his parents. He hoped the man was serious about leaving regardless of how many passengers were on board.

But when the driver reached the back of the bus, he smiled at his list.

"Thirty-eight souls aboard, all present and accounted for," he said. "Back to Dublin!"

It was still light when the coach reached O'Connell Street. The long, blue summer night stretched ahead of James like a prison sentence. He practically leapt off the coach, oblivious to the driver's broad grin, and made his way up the street to the Gresham Hotel, where he and Chloe had been staying.

He would leave Dublin first thing in the morning. He would be in a cab before dawn, on his way to the airport. But now, just now, he needed to think, needed to collect himself.

He stopped just outside the Gresham, its grand old façade a sane rebuke to the madness he had experienced in Glendalough. A beggar woman sitting on a filthy blanket was asking him for money in a faint, soft voice, and he ignored her until he heard her say his name.

"James, can't you help me? It's so dark down here," the woman said, looking at him with Chloe's face. But it was only half of her face; the rest had been pulled away, revealing red muscle beneath. Her eye popped out of her head and dribbled onto the pavement.

James screamed and fell back, wheeling his arms for balance. The early evening crowd passed him without a second look, but one of the doormen at the Gresham, a burly Catalan in a black uniform, spotted the interaction and rushed to James's aid.

"Is this person assailing you, sir?" the doorman asked.

James looked again, and Chloe was gone. The beggar was an old woman, her face ravaged by addiction and years spent sleeping rough, surrounded by the few possessions she had in the world.

"No..." James began, but the Catalan was already kicking the woman's belongings off her blanket and shouting at her to leave, prompting her to wail piteously in response.

James turned and crossed the broad boulevard, a passing car blaring its horn as it swerved around him. *You could get lost in the crowd in O'Connell Street*, James thought. That's what he needed, more than anything.

He came to the General Post Office and was relieved to see some kind of political demonstration taking place.

He stood at the edge of the gathering and tried to slow his breathing.

The entire crowd was made up of people who were either of pensionable age or barely out of their teens. A man with an accent that sounded more Scottish than Irish was droning on about something called the Legacy Bill. Behind him loomed a large poster with oval-shaped photographs of thin, staring faces and some slogan about the anniversary of a hunger strike.

So, we're back to that, he thought. *This is what passes for normal in this country. I won't spend a minute longer than I have to in this death-ridden madhouse.*

He turned to look at the people listening to the speaker and noticed a young man staring at him. For an instant, James had the absurd worry that the man could tell he was English just by looking at him.

And then, from underneath the young man's green jacket, a thicket of thin, white tendrils unspooled, landing on the pavement and snaking toward James, glowing faintly in the evening dark.

He gasped and pushed away from the crowd, running down one of the side streets off the great thoroughfare. The sun was setting now, and the shops and tourist stalls had mostly closed up. James slowed to a brisk walk and passed a corner where two police officers in high-vis vests were arguing with someone who might have been a street corner preacher or political madman.

The man was standing in front of a bedsheet stretched between two wooden poles on which he had painted a dense thicket of words in different colors and sizes. James could make out the words *limb from limb* and *spreading darkness* and *the eyes are upon us all.*

This must be a psychotic break, he thought. *Chloe must have fallen down a shaft or something in that cave, and this is my mind punishing me for not helping her, for planning to break it off, for never really loving her. Once I can sit and be calm, the world will regain its old shape.*

The early dinner crowd was out and moving through the streets. James arrived in front of a restaurant that had once been a church and went inside. Would he mind waiting thirty to forty minutes for a table? He would not. He stood outside and began to feel calmness creep over his body. His psychotic episode was over, or would be soon.

A walking tour stopped in front of the restaurant. Americans, he could tell: they were all so fat. The young Irishman leading the tour was talking about the history of the church, about the famous people who had been married or baptized there, about the church yard on the other side being converted into a city park.

"Now, the most famous person associated with this site is Theobald Wolfe Tone," the guide was telling the fat Americans. "Does anyone know that name? He was the leader of the United Irishmen, a group that staged an uprising against English rule in—"

My God, more of this, James thought. *Does it never end? Is there a single place in this country that doesn't have some zealot's blood sticking to it?*

He walked to the other side of the restaurant. He had plenty of time before he would be seated. He saw the park that had once been the graveyard of the church, and in the soft dusk it seemed cool and pleasant. There was no one else about except a young couple on one of the benches, sloppily kissing and pawing at one another. James was a little surprised to feel no stirring of desire, only embarrassment.

He paced across the trim green park, turning over possibilities for the next few days in his head. What would he tell people? He barely knew Chloe's parents, thank God, but he had to say *something*. He'd have to tell Liz something as well. Maybe he could say she took off with some strapping young Irish lad. Maybe people would even feel sorry for him, their misgivings about the relationship finally confirmed.

Don't feel bad, mate, she wasn't going to stay with someone practically her dad's age forever. Did she say how long she'd be gone, by any chance?

James reached the far end of the little park, the boundary marked by a building whose brick wall had been decorated with some kind of stone patchwork. He walked to get a closer look, and recoiled.

Tombstones. They were tombstones. They had taken the tombstones from the graveyard and built a wall with them.

James began to cry, his shoulders shaking in the fading light. The young couple on the bench had moved on, and he was alone in the park.

In front of him, the wall began to crumble.

The tombstones parted like teeth in a colossal mouth, and glowing white tendrils wrapped around his wrists and pulled him forward. He opened his mouth to scream, but tan, ridged arms plunged past his lips and teeth, reaching down into his body, pulling and tearing at his flesh and organs from within.

They dragged him into a void so dark that not even the light of the tendrils could illuminate it, and the wall snapped shut behind him, leaving the city to neither mourn nor miss the presence of one more harried stranger.

MARCELLA

Orrin Grey

Part of the deal that Marcella struck with her uncle in exchange for staying at the manor was that she be allowed to choose her own room. And so, on the day that the carriage deposited her outside the manor's big, wrought iron gate, she carried her luggage into the sweeping foyer. Her uncle said a distracted "hullo" from where he was arguing with a workman up on the landing and she left her bags to go explore the halls.

The manor house was built wide but not deep. The exterior walls were of a grey stone that appeared somehow green, possibly because the accents that surrounded them *were* green, as were the vines that crept verdant fingers across them. She thought about the green man figures she had seen surreptitiously carved on the lintels of churches, and of a green man so large that he could hold the manor in his hands, pulling it toward him for a kiss, or to be swallowed whole.

"Precocious" is what Marcella's parents had called her, when she was still a child and they were still alive. "Imaginative" is the word her uncle seemed to prefer. "Cheeky" or "impertinent" were more often employed by her teachers, when she had them.

The manor had once belonged to some Countess, whose final years and ultimate demise were apparently a great source of local legend. It was said that though the Countess was flaxen of hair and pale of eye herself, she had an affinity for her opposite, and surrounded herself in her waning years with young women, dark of hair and eye, whom she paid to be her servants and handmaidens. It was also said that the women and girls who worked at the house complained of illnesses and strange goings-on behind the doors of the manor, and sometimes fled in the night, refusing ever to return.

Marcella loved these stories. In part, because she was dark of hair and eye, but also because she could see through them to what she assumed was the truth of all the mystery: that the Countess had been a lesbian, and that everything from the illnesses to the "worse things" that went on behind the manor's closed doors were simply code for this secret.

When the Countess died, the manor became the property of the township, where the locals still whispered about the place and its former inhabitant. It would be very shivery to say that it remained empty because of the dark rumors that surrounded it, but in truth no one had the money to restore and keep up such a big, old house, at least until her uncle came along.

The manor had been the Countess's summer home, but she had retired here after her husband died, when the last years of her life were upon her. Marcella could see why. Out the back window there were gardens, now overgrown with creeping vines that nonetheless would broach night-blooming flowers. Out the front, a rain-swept vista of trees and crags led down to the town below. A beautiful, forbidding place, wild and tame all at once.

From the central foyer, the house primarily had two wings, which extended in a straight line in both directions. At each end, the wings turned at right angles into shorter halls that reached toward the back, cupping the gardens behind the house. Most of the doors were closed, and some stuck in their frames, forcing Marcella to put her shoulder against them and push to gain entry.

On the other side, she found rooms filled with the furniture that the Countess and her various ladies-in-waiting had left behind. Antiques that would probably have been worth a fortune to the right collector, all part of what her uncle had acquired when he paid the town's burgomaster a princely sum for the property.

The furnishings throughout showed what would have been considered a *woman's touch*, and yet there were also rooms that still smelled of pipe tobacco, and libraries filled with mouldering volumes on everything from Diogenes to the Battle of Marathon. Marcella ran her fingertips along the spines of the books, imagining the women that the Countess had gathered around her wearing smoking jackets and riding jodhpurs, drinking whiskey and smoking pipes, reading about philosophy and battles.

Everything had been dusted and cleaned scrupulously by a staff hired by her uncle. There was no dust on any surface, and while many of the books would probably still have to be thrown out, some seemed salvageable. There was also new furniture that had been brought in where the old had crumbled. Marcella struggled to tell the difference, because her uncle had purchased antiques dating from the same period, so that the transition would be as seamless as possible.

His plan was to transform the manor house into a resort. The intent was never for the two of them to live there permanently, but he wanted to be present for the repairs, the landscaping, and all of the other, innumerable decisions that went into such an undertaking. He had dragged Marcella along, though now that she was here, she was glad that she had left the city behind. This house had a poetry that their townhouse had never dreamed of.

From the moment that she opened the door to the room—the fifth down the hall, on the eastern wing—she knew that it would be hers. The bed that stood against the wall looked as if it had been caught in the midst of a transformation between bed and couch, with lemon-yellow cushions and pink linens and an elaborate frame of dark wood that reminded her of a ship's hull.

On the wall above the bed was a large, strange painting in which a nude woman lounged in some secluded spring or pool. The painting was in the Late Baroque style, the woman's figure all pink and plump, her breasts like peaches. The light was soft and touched with gold, the woman's flesh what all flesh aspires to, radiant with life.

Marcella had seen plenty of Rococo paintings before. What really drew her eyes to this one was that, instead of cherubs or woodland creatures, the woman was surrounded by grotesque fish, their scales bronze and steely green, their faces like an overdone mask of a fish, reminding her of a parade she had once seen when her uncle took her to Bali.

The rest of the room was pleasant. Leaded glass windows opened onto the garden beyond. There was a heavy writing desk, its wood finish stained with a slight green tinge. There was a dresser with its paint mostly worn away to reveal cherry wood beneath. But it was the bed and the painting that made Marcella fall in love.

"I found my room," she told her uncle as she passed him on the stair, getting up onto her tiptoes to give him a peck on his whiskery cheek.

"Good," was all he said, before returning to his argument.

It was not until that evening, as they ate dinner alone in the manor's large dining room, that her uncle told her about the room next to hers. It was the room on the corner, where the hall angled to wrap around the garden. Not the larger room that would be on the outside corner, but the smaller one, enclosed by the right angle of the hall.

"That was the Countess's room," he said around a forkful of Salisbury steak. "They say that she died in it. But that wasn't so unusual, in those days. Most people died at home. No, here's the interesting thing. When she granted the house to the town, she had one stipulation: that room must be sealed up and never touched. And it never has been, I'm told. It was even in the contract I signed to buy the place, with a hefty penalty should I violate the clause."

One of the reasons that Marcella enjoyed living with her uncle was that he entertained her morbid imagination. Where another adult might have attempted to shield her from such information, especially after she had already chosen the room next door, he knew that such a ghost story would only heighten her desire to sleep in the bed that nestled against the room's adjoining wall.

After dinner, when she went back to her room, Marcella stood in the hall outside the door to the Countess's old room. She put her palms against the wood, which felt no different than any other door in the house; no colder, no more alive. She pressed her ear to the panel but heard nothing. No whisper of ancient voices, no drip of cold blood. Finally, she got down, first to her hands and knees, and then flattening her chest against the floor, to peer through the gap beneath, but all she could see beyond was the dust that lay heavy on the floor of the chamber, undisturbed.

That night, Marcella saw the flowers blooming in the garden for the first time, whites and pinks, lavenders and the palest of blues. When the moon rose, she went for a walk along the overgrown paths, the breeze bringing their various scents to her. She could identify some of them, while others were alien.

She imagined—or imagined that she imagined—the laughter of nymphs carried on that same fragrant breeze. Closing her eyes, she dreamed the Countess's harem frolicking in the moonlight, their nightgowns more diaphanous than hers, revealing as much as they hid, teasing and tempting, smoothing and seducing.

She had left the light in her own room burning so she could look up and count one window to the east of it, finding the darkened rectangle of leaded glass that marked the Countess's room. She imagined the Countess standing vigil, her hair as pale as silk, as she watched her dark concubines play in the garden below.

The garden at that time would probably have looked quite different, but now it was overgrown in the extreme. The flowering vines loomed thick and close on all sides, their boughs hiding shadows as dark as the deepest cave. From within one, suddenly, there came a shaking, as the movement of some creature. It seemed enormous, like a tiger about to pounce upon her from the jungle. Marcella froze, her heart pounding in her chest, her blood turned to fire for a moment, when a fluffy grey housecat, no bigger than a breadbox, emerged from the shaking foliage.

The cat regarded her with liquid gold eyes that reflected like coins in the moonlight, and then it was gone beyond a garden wall.

Marcella returned to her room then, the garden's spell over her shattered by the cat's appearance, but the rush of that moment was not entirely gone from her blood. Her pores were alive with adrenaline, and as she lay in the dark, the moonlight streaming in through the leaded glass, her hands slipped down her body, hiking up the hem of her nightgown.

She thought of the tiger she had imagined leaping upon her, its jaws red with her blood.

That night, she had the dream for the first time. She was lying in her bed—*this* bed, in this room, with the moonlight spilling in and her nightgown still gathered around one hand, as she had fallen asleep when she finished—and she knew, in the dream, that she was asleep, although she could also see what was happening.

A shadow gathered at the foot of the bed, deepening even though nothing else in the room moved. From the shadow came first a huge, hairy grey paw, which placed itself softly upon the foot of the bed, flexing claws like darning needles to dig into the covers that were piled there. In the darkness beyond, two golden orbs appeared, as the huge grey cat dragged itself onto the bed.

Had she been awake, Marcella would have recognized the giant beast as a subconscious jumbling of the cat she had seen in the garden and her fantasies about the tiger. In the dream, however, she could see it for nothing but what it was, as it crept over her paralyzed form, its breath hot on her breasts, on her throat.

Marcella woke in the sunlight, her sheets damp and tangled about her. Her mouth was cottony, and in her muscles was the pleasant ache that follows enjoyable exertion. Her nightgown had slid uncomfortably off one shoulder, exposing one of her breasts. Someone was knocking on the door, an unfamiliar voice—belonging, presumably, to one of the various staff that her uncle had crawling about the estate during daytime hours—calling to tell her that breakfast was ready.

Over the next several days and weeks, Marcella had the same dream almost every night. On the rare occasion that she didn't dream of the great, grey cat, another haunted her, albeit with less frequency. She floated in the hall outside her own room. All the doors were closed and dark, except the one next to hers, the one that led to the sealed chamber. It was open, spilling golden light and soft music into the hall.

As she drifted to the door, she heard voices mixing with the music. The voices of women, all talking together, laughing. She could never make out the words. They poured over her like rain, but there was something unstudied in them. These were the words that you said in the deep watches of the night, when your tongue had been loosed by drink or by drugs. Unguarded words, spoken not necessarily from the heart, but from the yearning part of you that longed to be seen but also dreaded it, in the daytime world. Words spoken with a freedom that few ever got to experience.

Beyond the door, the room was bigger than was possible. Inside, it was somehow every room in the house. Marcella recognized books and furnishings from countless chambers that she had passed through. There were also women and girls. To a one, they were dark of hair and eye, though Marcella was not likely to get lost among them, for her hair was bobbed short and curly, while most of theirs hung straight past their shoulders.

Some lounged on pillows and sheets, some toyed with one-another's ebon locks. Some ate, some drank, some smoked, some read, some played on instruments that Marcella could not name. Some wore gowns and jewels, some were dressed in clothes that the servants would have worn in decades past, while others sported men's clothing, tuxedos and smoking jackets. All looked comfortable, as though they wore only what they wished. Some that lounged upon the divans and beds in the room wore nothing at all, their skin smooth, their bushes as dark as the hair on their heads, hiding and tantalizing in equal measure.

Outside the window, more figures were in the garden, their white, sheer nightgowns making them flash and glow like flowers that bloomed in the dark.

The path of her dream did not allow her to linger, however. It turned her inexorably toward the wall that this impossible room shared with her own. There, the Countess waited. She was tall and regal, but also pale and drawn. She stood beside a wardrobe, which was carved with images of strange fish. And as she opened the door onto darkness, she gestured for Marcella to come inside.

Sometime during her second week at the manor, she walked into town. Her uncle was meeting contractors back at the estate, and she decided to "get some air." She walked down the dirt path leading from the front gates of the manor house to the little hamlet at the bottom of the hill, with its cobbled streets and quaint shops. Here was an occasionally uncomfortable juxtaposition of old and new; while much of the town looked as it probably had when the Countess dwelt in the house above, Marcella had to step into a doorway to avoid a passing motor truck that was too wide for the narrow streets.

It was only when she had passed part of the day in town, eating outside a small café and watching birds squabble over her crumbs, and was headed back toward the manor, that she noticed the people staring. At first, she assumed that it was because she was new to the area, or because they knew that she was associated with the money that had come to buy the Countess's old abode. But then, as she was leaving the last of the little houses behind, she turned back and saw the actual reason for their odd looks: she was being trailed by a dozen or more cats, what must have been every tom and molly in the area.

They followed until she was nearly to the gates of the manor, never getting any closer, but also never turning away. Even after she had passed onto the grounds of the estate, the cats sat on their haunches out in the road and watched, though they were gone when she brought her uncle to the window to look.

The same morbid imagination that made Marcella relish her room meant that she had read plenty of ghost stories. She even learned enough German to make her way through a book of them that her uncle had brought back from one of his travels. So, she knew that the things she had been experiencing in the house were unusual, long before she caught her reflection in the mirror and saw how drawn she was looking. The coloration of her skin had changed, and she was thin, her cheek bones visible beneath the layer of baby fat that had always defined the shape of her face.

She looked like she hadn't been sleeping, when in fact the exact opposite was true. Each day, she went to bed earlier, and slept in later, and she had read enough stories to know that, sooner or later, she would stop leaving her bed altogether. As it was, she lay in it before drifting off to sleep, or after she had been called to breakfast in the morning, and stared up at the plump, vibrant woman in the painting. Did her cheeks seem even rosier than they had before? Her breasts riper?

By the time the drop of blood appeared from behind the gilded frame and slowly streaked its way across the wallpaper, down to the bed itself, Marcella already knew what she would find when she pushed the corner of the painting aside. Even then, it took a massive effort to stir herself to do so, or to care when she saw what she had known it would reveal: a rectangle of blood, staining the wall like a sponge.

Would even that have been enough to stir her to action, had it not been for the dream? Her fingertips trailing the blood from the painting, smearing it across her cheek, her thigh, Marcella slumped back onto the couch-like bed. Pushing aside the frame had been all she was capable of in that moment, and she fell into a deep sleep, during which she dreamed a third dream, different from any that she had experienced before.

It began on the road leading down to the village. Night had long since fallen, but the moon was bright. Marcella drifted yet again, as she did in the dreams of the Countess's room. She traveled down the road without touching the ground, until she came to the window of a small house. Light shone from inside, and as she drifted up to the panes, she saw a young woman beyond, bathing herself in a claw-footed tub. As the woman scooped up water and poured it over her shoulders and neck, Marcella rapped her knuckles against the glass.

The woman looked up. She was Marcella's opposite in many ways. Her skin was freckled from time spent working in the sun and her hair was the color of straw. When she locked eyes with the stranger outside her window, however, she smiled. Heedless of her nakedness—or proud of it—she rose from the bath and walked to the portal, unlatching it so that Marcella could lean in. She tasted the minerals of the water on their kiss, and then she tasted blood.

The dream became fragmented after that, but Marcella retained the image that had been the last she saw before waking. Her own reflection in the mirror downstairs, her eyes shining gold coins, her mouth smeared with red.

At first, Marcella's uncle was reluctant to open the Countess's old room. He had signed a contract, after all, and its fiduciary penalties were steep. When she showed him the rectangle of blood on the wall above her bed, however, his hesitation vanished. Two of the contractors helped to break down the door, for no key had been included in the estate.

The chamber on the other side was disappointing. No larger than it should have been, it was coated in a thick layer of dust, and absent any furnishings whatsoever, save for a single ornate wardrobe, carved with nautical fauna. When the door was opened, Marcella's uncle turned to her, where she stood resolute in the hall, and she pointed to the wardrobe. Even before they pulled it open, they could smell the blood. It had pooled on the bottom of the cabinet, and across the entire back of the wardrobe was a bloody stain, its shape that of a human figure.

Years later, Marcella wrote an article about her experience in the room. It turned into a book deal with a small university press. The book never sold particularly well, but it fed into the mania for scholarly works on vampirism that was going around at the time.

She had wanted to call the book *The Picture on the Wall*, which had been the title of her original article, but her publisher had insisted upon *The Bloody Portrait*, in the interest of marketing, and Marcella eventually capitulated. Her girlfriend at the time told her that it was a better title anyway. She was probably right.

Marcella left the manor after the Countess's room was opened, but her uncle owned it for many more years. The wardrobe and the painting were burned in the garden out behind the house, and the Countess's old room was used for storage, not as a guest room. No one who stayed at the resort ever complained of anemia or nocturnal visits. Before Marcella's uncle died, he sold the place at a considerable profit.

Marcella never went back, but the dreams still came. Not every night, not even every week, but often. Dreams of the great, grey cat, creeping its way up her bed, its breath hot on her breasts, on her throat. Dreams of women and girls, dancing together beneath the moonlight, Marcella among them. And when they came, she welcomed them.

SLAY AT HOME MOM

Christa Carmen

Our Three Weeks in Renovations Hell, an update on the kiddos, and some BIG NEWS!!!

Catlynn Heron 117K subscribers
11K views, 2 weeks ago, 9 products

⏵ The house's interior in the background is all muted greys and pale teal. A grey couch outfitted with waffle weave blankets and carefully arranged throw pillows is visible in the far-left frame. A round, rattan pendant lamp offers soft, complimentary lighting on the two figures in the frame.

Time lapse video of a thin, blonde woman applying makeup as a baby mouths blocks on the floor beside her. A "View Products" button appears; clicking it brings up a $40 lengthening mascara, $27 eyebrow gel, and a $60 eyeshadow palette. The time lapse video stops, and our host stands and walks to the front of the room. Several Montessori-style children's toys—a play kitchen set, woven baskets full of sensory boards and handheld percussion instruments—fill the frame in the background. The baby crawls toward the toys, trying—and failing—to liberate a barn from a basket. The baby looks to her mother, but her mother's attention is on the camera in front of her.

Catlynn Heron's voice is slightly drawling, a touch of a Midwestern accent rounding the corners of her words.

> CATLYNN HERON
> Oh my god, you guys, this week! It has just been crazy. As you can see, we're starting to settle in after all the renovations. Little Beanie is loving the wall-to-wall carpeting in the new playroom.

Catlynn gestures to the baby without turning around. The makeup still sits on the corner of an end table beside a vase of butter-yellow daylilies. The baby pulls herself up to stand, her chubby-fingered hands exploring the table's surface. Upon finding the mascara, she plops back onto her diapered rear and puts the tube into her mouth.

> CATLYNN
> Though, I could move Beanie out to the woods, and as long as she had, like, pinecones to play with—and Mama's milk, of course— she'd be totally content. Remember you guys, you can check out these amazing nursing tanks from Sweet Angel Baby Face Maternity Gear. I have just been *living* in them!

Catlynn runs her hands down the sleek, hunter-green top she wears.

> CATLYNN
> So, as I was saying, we're all settled in, even Miss Zippy.

Dissolve to: Interior, A Little Girl's Bedroom

CATLYNN
Zippy is *thriving*. I totally thought she was
going to hate the fact that we had to stay with
her grandparents for three weeks, but she
loved it. I mean, *of course* they spoiled her
rotten. Check out the new DIY journal sets
they showered her with, and that Zippy just
adores. We're totally going to keep these in
stock for, like, ever.

The camera pans right and Catlynn stands before a pink-
adorned girl with her mother's same long blonde hair,
scribbling in a faux-fur journal, a unicorn horn sticking up
from the top of the back cover.

ZIPPY
Can we get more of these awesome glitter
markers?

CATLYNN
Of course, honey! And, you guys, for me, it
was totally nice to spend time with my
parents too. I haven't seen them in forever,
but I'll say this. And this is between me and
you...

Catlynn giggles and the camera zooms in on her face, as if
she's about to share a secret.

CATLYNN
...well, between me and all one-hundred-
seventeen-thousand of you. But while I
haven't seen my parents in a long time, I
haven't seen my sister in even longer. She
moved to Germany two years ago, intent on
exploring the whole Germanic pagan

movement or something equally crazy. She
and I got into an argument before she left. I
called her, like, a demon lover or witch
groupie or something stupid; she was always
falling for these tall, dark, messed up dudes—
I may have even teased her that she'd try to
bed the devil himself—and she overreacted.
Besides the occasional text, we haven't been
communicating much since she left the states.
But...

The camera zooms out; Catlynn is back in the living room.
She wears an oversized t-shirt over sleek black leggings. The
"View Products" button appears on-screen again. The
camera zooms back in.

CATLYNN
...my parents told me that Annetta—that's my
sister—is pregnant! Like, can you believe that,
you guys? She goes and gets pregnant in
Germany with some guy who, of course,
neither me nor my parents have ever met,
and she doesn't even tell me! Not only that,
but apparently she's due any day! I'm going to
be the bigger person and give her a call,
because how can she be the sister of one of
the most successful Mom-bloggers out there
and not take my advice? I need to hear all the
details of this pregnancy! I need to have her
on my channel! I need to—

Zippy steps into the frame, arms full of dolls and accessories.

ZIPPY
Can you help me set up my fort away from
Beanie so I can play?

CATLYNN (over her shoulder)
Sure, honey.

Cut to: time lapse video of Catlynn dragging a fairy tale-style tent to the center of the playroom. The "View Products" button is back. Catlynn secures a baby gate within the door frame, lifts a wailing Beanie from the floor, and carries her to the kitchen, where she places her in a futuristic-looking high chair.

CATLYNN
All right, friends, families, and casual followers. Time to cook dinner then get these girls to bed. After that, I'm going to pour myself a big glass of rosé, settle in on the new couch, and...

Catlynn brings her hands to her chest.

CATLYNN
...call my sister! I'll post a video to let you guys know how it goes! Until then, be your best selves, your own biggest supporters, and the strongest advocates for what your kiddos need. Love you!

The Doctor Mommy Blog

A pediatrician's—and mother's—guide to healthier, happier children

Quick Links:
Immunity, Medication, Viral Illnesses | Mental Health | School | Practical Tips | Safe Summer Fun |Travel | Sleep

09/06/23: The Toughest Role a Pediatrician Ever Has to Play... the Mandated Reporter

Hi there, dedicated moms, dads, and caregivers. Dr. Bruer here, with the most difficult subject I've written about to date. Most caregivers won't ever have to concern themselves with this, but for those who find themselves the subject of an investigation by a government agency tasked with keeping children safe from abuse and neglect, I want to try to shed light on this difficult topic.

Now, I know I have a lot of English-speaking subscribers to my blog here in Germany, but as an expat with a large following based in the United States, I want to give a brief overview of the differences in reporting between the two countries, after which I'll share my experience with this topic, and why I'm at a bit of a loss at present, personally and professionally speaking.

In the US, there are certain professions— mental health professionals, clergy, police, teachers, and, of course, pediatricians and other doctors—mandated by law to report child maltreatment. If an individual in one of these professions suspects neglect or physical, psychological, emotional, or sexual abuse, they are to submit a report to law enforcement or their local public health agency.

In Germany, where I've lived and worked for the past nine years, the expectation is quite different. Doctors here are *not* legally obligated to report cases where they suspect child abuse and neglect. They *are permitted* to report their suspicions to child protective services or to the police, but again, *they are not obligated and will suffer no legal consequences should they chose to ignore signs of abuse or neglect.*

Which brings me to my current conundrum, and a clear example of how slippery it can be to navigate these situations, not just from a legal standpoint, but from an ethical one. A woman—I'll call her Grace—recently requested, and met requirements for, a home birth, but was scheduled to bring her infant into my office for U1 and U2 (the first two of nine mandatory examinations, called U-Untersuchungen) the day after delivering. She never showed. Each time we called to reschedule, her phone would go to voicemail. When we sent her paperwork via post, it came back undeliverable.

Now, the woman could have decided against a home birth, and delivered at another hospital. As an expat herself, she could even have returned to the states, though with a no-fly policy after thirty-six weeks on practically every airline, the timing would have been tight. But when I reached out to Grace's obstetrician, the file they sent over gave every indication that Grace had been intent on a home birth. Regardless of my unease over the apparent disappearance of this woman and her newborn, there didn't seem to be much more I could do.

That is, until I stepped into the elevator of my apartment complex this past Tuesday evening and hit the button for my floor. Before the doors could close, a woman's voice called from the lobby.

"Could you hold, please?" And then, "Err, könntest du bitte halten?" I stuck my arm out to keep the doors from closing. And who should step in but the woman from the photograph atop the medical folder on my desk back at my office: Grace.

She gave me a tired half-smile and rested her shopping bags on the floor. I saw baby formula, newborn diapers, and a baggie from the butcher shop. When Grace directed her attention to the rapidly changing numbers above the door, I leaned over to get a better look. The sticker on the baggie read "Hühnerherzen." Chicken hearts. Strange, but not the oddest of postpartum cravings I've seen. Grace got off on the thirty-sixth floor. I stuck my head out and watched her put her key in the door for an apartment halfway down the hall. Then, I rode up to the forty-second floor, wondering if I should have told her who I was.

I've always promised to be nothing but honest in these posts. And I do swear that I only rode back down to the thirty-sixth floor an hour later out of worry for the baby, a baby who very well may have been kept from his first—and mandatory—checkup with medical professionals. But it felt like prying as I crept to the apartment she'd gone to, #3604, and worse when I pressed my ear to the door. I heard a baby wailing, and my breathing quickened. *Relax*, I told myself. *Babies cry all the time.* But then I heard something I've been trying to make sense of every night since: strange, guttural growls, followed by a series of crashing blows, like a body being thrown against a wall. I froze. Blood throbbed in my temples. I didn't know what to do.

I stood there, thoughts racing, wondering if I should knock, pretend to have been passing by, ask Grace if she needed help. There was silence for several moments, followed by ragged gasps and frantic mewling. I was about to turn away, when a new sound drifted out of #3604. Grace was singing a lullaby, and while the tune was familiar, the words had been altered in ways that sent goosebumps rippling up my arms and across my neck:

> Hush little darling, don't you cry,
> Mama knows you wouldn't hurt a fly.
> I'll buy what you long for, iron and slick,
> We'll fill your tummy nice and quick.
> And if that sustenance doesn't appeal
> Mama will find you another meal.
> And if that meal doesn't soothe your soul,
> We'll take what we need and dig a hole.
> And if its contents won't stay buried,
> Mama won't worry, she won't be harried.
> We'll take what we need underneath the moon,
> Then tuck ourselves away in our safe cocoon.
> Hush little pup, hush my little pet,
> I'll keep you safe from the world's dark threats.

Somehow, I made it back to my own apartment, where I picked up my phone, planning to call the police. The more I thought about it, however, the more I wasn't sure of what I'd heard. Or what I thought I knew. It still stood that Grace could have delivered elsewhere and the baby had been seen by medical professionals. That Grace was just doing what she could to calm her child. The crashing could have been a television left on in the background, the strange lullaby a way for a sleep-deprived mother to amuse herself on a difficult night.

Still, I've always trusted my medical intuition, and I can't shake the feeling that something's wrong. I don't *have* to call the authorities on the suspicion that Grace has neglected to provide medical care for her son. I'm not *obligated* to let the police know of the strange sounds coming from the apartment. But should I?

More soon...

Dr. Abigail Bruer, MD

Beanie's first steps, making time for ME, and an update on
my sister in Germany!!!

Catlynn Heron 119.5K subscribers
597K views, 3 days ago, 4 products

▶ Zippy and Catlynn are kneeling, each with a hand on
the side of a tottering Beanie, a wide grin on her open,
drool-soaked mouth.

CATLYNN (to Zippy)
Okay, sweetheart, take your hand away. Let's
see if she'll do it again.

Zippy and Catlynn cease helping Beanie balance. The baby
wavers, then careens forward in a series of jerky, uneven
steps. Catlynn cheers, startling Beanie, who tips forward
onto the carpet. The camera cuts to Catlynn alone in the
kitchen.

CATLYNN
You guys, I'm so proud of my little Bean. I
know I usually post once a week, but I had to
share the news about our littler walker. That,
and a wild update about what's going on with
my sister. I know a record number of you—
resulting in nearly two thousand new
subscribers...

Catlynn presses her hands together in exaggerated gratitude.

CATLYNN
...tuned in to watch my first phone call to my
sister since finding out she's pregnant, and
you guys, you know how I was so distraught
after the call? I mean, here's Annetta, alone in

Germany, a new, and apparently single, mom—can you say, "hashtag-deadbeat-dad-alert?"—and all I hear in the background while we're talking is her baby crying, and Annetta sounded so distracted, dodging half my questions, totally giving the impression that she hasn't slept at all since having this baby. Well, I cannot believe I'm saying this but American Airlines reached out and offered to pay my way to Frankfurt so I can see my sister in person, meet her little bundle of joy, and feature her on my channel! It will be just like one of those nineties rom-com makeover movies, only with an in-over-her-head mom and obsolete nursing bras instead of, like, a geeky girl in glasses. I cannot wait, and I want each and every one of you to go on this journey with me!

Cutaway to a graphic of a plane flying from the US to Germany over a colorful world map. The camera returns to Catlynn in her bedroom, placing clothes in a large suitcase.

CATLYNN
Before you guys go crazy asking in the comments, no, I haven't told Annetta I'm coming, but I got her address from my parents, and she doesn't watch my channel, so my visit will be a big surprise! Annetta has always been anti-social media—except for that time she joined that pagan, or, black-candle-lovers-united, dating site, and I never let her hear the end of it—but before we had that stupid fight, we were always close. Well, close-ish. And she sounded so exhausted

when we spoke. I mean, I know she said she was fine, and that she was loving motherhood, but we used to raise our babies in literal villages, you guys. She doesn't even know how much she needs me. Until then, be your best selves, your own biggest supporters, and the strongest advocates for what your kiddos need. *Auf Wiedersehen!*

POLICE REPORT
(Pursuant to Code 11666)

To Be Completed by Intake Officer
Date: 12-Sep-2023

Case Number: 458903

(Translated for distribution to Massachusetts State Police, United States)

US Contact: Det. Brian Furlong

Translator: Hilda Müller

A. Missing Party

Name: Abigail Bruer   **Title:** Dr.

Address: 146 Oberdorfelder Straße 4211 OG · 61138 Niederdorfelden

Business/Agency: Neropädiatrische Suiten

Address: Theodor-W.-Adorno Platz 17 · 60323 Frankfurt

Telephone: 069/6301–7177

Did Anyone Witness the Incident: ☐ YES ☒ NO

B. Incident Information

If necessary, attach extra sheet(s) or other form(s) and check this box ☐

Date/Time of Incident: Friday, Sept. 08, 2023

Place of Incident: 146 Oberdorfelder Straße 3604 OG ·
61138 Niederdorfelden

**Narrative Description (where missing was last seen,
by whom, color and type of clothing missing was
known to be wearing, etc.):**

Last seen by coworkers leaving the pediatric offices of
Neropädiatrische Suiten, alone, in black pants, a white
blouse, and small silver hoop earrings. Requests to check
in on the missing woman came from followers of her
Facebook page and popular pediatric blog, "Doctor
Mommy" after Abigail Bruer stated she planned to look
in on a client who hadn't shown up for her newborn's
medical visits. Dr. Bruer's family has initiated a missing
person's report in her home state of Massachusetts,
United States.

Catlynn Heron
909 Following | **59.2K** Followers | **790K** Likes
Wife ✦ Mom to 2 amazing kiddos ✦ Homemaker
▢ Blogger
Link.branches: CatlynnHeron

Short Video Transcript, 09/09/2023:

You guys, I'm in Germany! I'm staying at the gorgeous Hotel Amadeus Frankfurt, a short drive from my sister's apartment complex. It's lovely here. The flight went smoothly, I just checked in with Paul, and he says that Beanie and Zippy [Catlynn blows kisses at the camera] miss Mommy terribly but are doing just fine. I'm going to get settled in, have my first taste of German cuisine, then grab a rideshare over to Annetta's place in a couple of hours. Make sure you tune in to my live feed over on YouTube at eight p.m. sharp to see our reunion!

POLICE REPORT ADDENDUM

Case Number: 458903

The following is a printout of an unfinished blog post discovered on A. Bruer's laptop. Post is dated the same as that of her disappearance; timestamp of blog creation is 19:30 (UTC+2).

The Doctor Mommy Blog

A pediatrician's—and mother's—guide to healthier, happier children

09/08/2023: Something's not right here

I'm in my apartment, trying to decide what to do. I went back to "Grace's" place, and things are…she is…something is going on with that woman, but I'm not sure if she needs a police intervention or a mental health one. I had this blog draft up to work on a new post later, but I'm going to use it now to try to make sense of what I just saw. I couldn't get Grace and her baby out of my head, not to mention that unnerving lullaby I'd heard her singing from behind the door, so I went to her apartment after work, thinking I'd just be honest: introduce myself as her baby's intended pediatrician, tell her I realized we lived in the same building, and ask how things were going. Grace was home, and answered the door politely, but that's where any normalcy ended. She invited me in, and I followed her back through a darkened apartment. Instantly, the smell of the shadowy rooms hit me: a rank, dizzying smell of iron and cloying, sickly sweet rot. The windows were obscured by thick, claustrophobia-inducing curtains.

She hesitated at an open doorway, beyond which I could just make out the glimmer of appliances, but she seemed to change her mind about entering the kitchen, and instead turned right, into a living room.

"Please," she said, gesturing at a chair. Her voice was distant, distracted. "How can I help you, Dr. Bruer?"

I explained the reason for my visit, my own voice quavering more than I would've liked. I suddenly felt it was a bad idea to have come here, not just due to the inherent creepiness of the place, the air of *wrongness* hanging over everything. But because my concerns, even with the horrible smell and drawn curtains, still seemed flimsy at best, nosy at worst. Grace nodded when she heard my spiel, but said nothing. She stared off in the direction of the hallway, at a closed door opposite the living room. She stared so silently and for so long, I finally stood up.

"I'm sorry to have disturbed you," I said. "I'll leave you be."

Grace put a hand up. "No," she said flatly. "I'm glad you came. Let me get you something from the kitchen." She took a few steps forward then spun back to face me. "Tea, I mean. Some biscuits." I started to refuse, but she disappeared from the room.

Five minutes passed. Then another five. I heard rustling, the occasional bang. Then, a plopping noise, followed by an extended hiss. I crept into the hallway. The smell there had gotten worse. Thicker. It was hard to breathe. Gathering my courage, I stepped into the kitchen.

It was a veritable abattoir in there. Blood streaked the stove and sides of the refrigerator, and splatters patterned the white tile above the sink, even going as high as the wall above the backsplash in places. It dripped down the cabinets and darkened the hardwood floor. A large pot on the stove bubbled over, the pink-tinged water pooling on the stove top. Grace stood before it, ladle in hand, then turned when she heard me enter the room.

I tried to hold her gaze, but my attention was drawn to the plates. Plates on every surface of every table and counter in the kitchen. Plates full of bloody livers, hearts, gizzards, piles of chopped meat, ropes of intestine. Blood-stained plastic baggies from the butcher shop spilled from the trashcan and onto the floor.

I mumbled something between an entreaty and an apology. Grace studied me with interest.

"The baby," I managed to get out. "Where is your baby? Is he okay?"

Grace smiled reverently. "Of course," she said. "Like any first-time mother, it took me a bit to get used to things. Learn his preferences, sleep schedule, how he likes to be soothed." Her eyes flashed with something like pride. "How to feed him."

I backed several steps out of the kitchen as a noise rose above the bubbling of the pots on the stove. Grace returned to stirring the viscous concoction, and I ran. Out of her apartment, past the elevator, and up twelve flights of stairs to my own door. I've been sitting here ever since, hands trembling as I type. I fear, in my haste to get inside, I may have left the door to my apartment unlocked. But I can't get it out of my head. The noise I heard. From the room off the hall. Some mixture of helpless mewling, tiny coos, and a deep, guttural growl. I can hear it. Even now. From as close as the next room.

That, and snatches of a lullaby. I need to

Comments: The landlord for #3604 could not be reached at the time of this report.

Signature of Officer Completing Report: *Elias Pichler*

<u>WATCH LIVE – Reunited (with my sister and her new baby!)</u>
<u>and it feels so good!!!</u>

37K watching | Started 4m ago
#mommyblogger... more
Catlynn Heron 123K subscribers

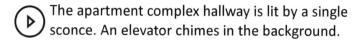 The apartment complex hallway is lit by a single
sconce. An elevator chimes in the background.

Catlynn stands in front of #3604. She's holding the camera so
it's aimed at her face. She fixes her viewers with a furtive
grin.

CATLYNN HERON
You guys, I'm here. This is her door.

Catlynn presses her ear to dark wood and listens, then turns
back to the camera.

CATLYNN
I'm going to put the camera down until I get
inside. Once Annetta gets over her shock at
seeing me, and I'm all the way in, I'll find a
place to prop the phone. That way, you guys
can see her shock turn to gratitude when I
explain to her that I'm not just here as her
sister but in official mommy-blogger capacity.
If things were as rough as they sounded over
the phone, she's going to be so relieved!
Okay, here we go.

The picture goes fuzzy, then refocuses on Catlynn's pant leg.
A knock sounds on the door. Silence. Another knock. More
silence. Then, footsteps. The door creaks open.

UNKNOWN VOICE
Can I help you?

CATLYNN
Annetta!

ANNETTA (after a pause)
Catlynn? What the hell are you doing here?

Catlynn laughs lightly.

CATLYNN
Oh, you know. Can I come in?

ANNETTA
Seriously, Catlynn, what the hell?

A moment of silence, then the door creaks again, as if
Annetta is peering into the hallway, checking in either
direction. She sighs.

ANNETTA
Fine, come in. Come in and tell me what the
hell you're doing in Germany.

Footsteps. The door creaks closed. A whir of movement and
the camera focuses on Catlynn. She makes a face that says,
I'm in! and continues following a dark-haired woman down
the hall. The camera returns to her side, tracking her
progress as they turn right and cross a threshold into an unlit
room.

CATLYNN
Can we turn a light on? Why is it so dark in
here?

Fingers scratch against the phone's speaker. The camera faces out into a dimly lit room. Annetta's back is to the phone, which allowed Catlynn the chance to prop it somewhere. There's a click, and the picture brightens. Catlynn is visible in profile, angled toward the dark-haired, pale-faced woman.

> ANNETTA
> Okay, you're inside. You've got your light. Now, what are you doing here?

> CATLYNN (lightly)
> Is that any way to speak to the sister who traveled almost five thousand miles to see you?

> ANNETTA
> It is when the visit is unexpected. And unwelcome.

> CATLYNN
> Jesus, Annetta, I came to help you after Mom and Dad said you were having a baby! Speaking of which, where is he?

Catlynn leans forward to peer across the hallway, but Annetta steps to the side, blocking the door.

> ANNETTA
> I don't need your help. I don't need anyone's help.

> CATLYNN
> Of course you do! Everyone needs help. And I can give you the kind of help that not just anyone is privy to.

ANNETTA
Why is that? Because of your blog? Because
of your selfish, unethical, disgusting blog?

Annetta takes two steps to the right, her expression blank
and unreadable. Catlynn blinks and licks her lips. Her eyes
dart to the camera but flick back quickly to her sister's face.

CATLYNN
I'm a good mother.

ANNETTA
You don't know the first thing about being a
good mother.

Annetta takes two more steps to the right, forcing Catlynn to
take two steps of her own, toward the door.

ANNETTA (continues)
How about protecting your children, for one?
Affording them a measure of privacy? How
about giving them what they need, no matter
what? How about not projecting your own,
self-serving needs onto them and pretending
it's for their benefit? What do your children
need, Catlynn? What do they need? Do you
ever give it to them? Despite what you want?
That's the mark of a good mother. Sacrifice.
Doing whatever it takes, no matter the cost.
No matter the strife. No matter the mess. No
matter the blood, sweat, and tears. The
blood. No matter the smell.

CATLYNN (whispering)
What are you talking about, Annetta? What
blood? Can't we just, like, take a look at some

of the products I brought you? I thought if
you just let me show you—

ANNETTA (looking directly into the camera)
You think I don't see you trying to pull us into
your sphere of narcissistic madness? I moved
here to get away from all of that. From you.

CATLYNN (indignantly)
I think you moved here to satisfy your creepy
interest in, like, dark shit. Paul and I are
raising Beanie and Zippy with values. We take
them to church.

ANNETTA (laughing)
Like that can undo the god-awful behavior
you model for them.

CATLYNN
Oh, and raising your child without his father is
somehow better?

ANNETTA
I got everything I needed from my son's
father; don't you worry about that. And I
won't be cowed into swallowing down
society's expectations for single mothers. I
can promise you—promise you—that my son
will achieve things in his lifetime your children
wouldn't even comprehend.

Annetta directs her attention to the camera again.

ANNETTA (continues)
Things their social media-addled brains
cannot conceive.

Annetta's lips curl into a 1000-watt smile.

CATLYNN (sniffling, sounding fearful)
Annetta, please. Let me turn off the video,
then we can talk without—

ANNETTA
Oh, we're turning off the video. The last thing
I want is my son exposed to that evil shit.

Annetta's hand obscures the lens. There's the scratchy sound
of fingers against the speaker, but beneath that, a low
whine, rising to a guttural, choppy growl. The growl
increases in volume and intensity. Someone shrieks, and an
explosion of glass drowns everything else out. A moment of
silence, and then...

CATLYNN (unintelligibly)
Stop...it's not, it's not...

The screen goes dark.

IndyStar

PUBLIC SAFETY

'She Just Vanished': Indiana Influencer Goes Missing After Traveling to Germany to Visit Sister

Police and the family of a 25-year-old woman who went missing in Germany are asking for help locating her.

Catlynn Heron was last seen at 146 Oberdorfelder Straße in the municipality of Niederdorfelden, on Sept. 9, said her mother Natalia Daniels.

Heron lived with her husband, Paul, and two daughters, ages 6 and 1, in Indianapolis.

"Her purpose in life is her daughters," Daniels said. "And her work as an influencer. I don't know what else to say except that this is not normal."

Before she went missing, Heron traveled to Germany on a flight sponsored by American Airlines to film a reunion episode between her and her previously estranged sister on Heron's YouTube channel.

Heron is 5 feet and 3 inches tall, weighs 112 pounds and has blonde hair and blue eyes. Anyone with information on her whereabouts should contact the Hesse State Police in Germany or the Indianapolis Metropolitan Police Department.

r/CatlynnHeron Lounge

A place for members of r/CatlynnHeron to chat with each other

⬆ 55 ⬇ | ⬭ 2.9K | ⬆ Share

+ Add a Comment

Brightgreeneyes 5 days ago

Everyone commenting on this forum is missing the most important issue. Yes, Catlynn Heron is ALL over the news. Yes, her disappearance is being treated as legitimate. And yes, the US Embassy is now involved in trying to locate her. But NO ONE is focusing on Catlynn's last YouTube livestream. I mean, Catlynn admitted her sister was into some dark shit before traveling to see her, and the details around Annetta moving to Germany in the first place are bizarre. Then there's the weird shit with no one in the family knowing who the baby daddy is. AND THERE WAS A STRUGGLE at the end of the YouTube video. Granted, the video was up for less than a minute after it posted, but people saw that shit. Something happened in that apartment, and the authorities are not nearly as focused on that as they should be, IMO.

Influencemebabee 3 days ago

@Brightgreeneyes, YOU are the one hyper-focusing on the wrong things here. My brother's best friend's cousin is on the IndyMetro PD and he says the apartment in Niederdorfelden wasn't rented to an Annetta Daniels...it wasn't rented to ANYONE. And why the family hasn't reported BOTH sisters missing? Something fishy there...

Ambitiousblogbait 1 day ago

The lack of info on the sister is worrisome. The lack of focus on the struggle that took place during Catlynn's livestream is equally troubling. But I was up that night. I watched the footage. And I haven't been able to sleep since. Because I saw something on that video far more frightening than whatever happened between Catlynn and her sister, pagan or not, interested in the occult or not. It was in the background of the video, in the room across the hall. If you looked really closely, you could just make out what appeared to be the slats of a crib in the darkness. Catlynn was there to help her sister with her new baby, right? So a crib makes sense. But there was something in that crib. Something that wasn't a sleeping baby. At first I thought it was like, one of those stuffed animals that shoot stars on the wall or something, to help get a fussy infant to sleep. But it was wrong. All wrong. There were just two lights, somehow dim and piercing at the same time. And the color...the color was greenish black, but a bit yellow, too. Like a sickly version of the Northern Lights or something. But situated in an oval of black shadow.

They were eyes. Sick, staring, yellowy-green-black eyes. Staring out from between slats in the crib at what was going on in the living room. Waiting.

Lindau Neighborhood Watch [translated from German]

About this group

Let us all know what is happening in our neighborhood and help each other. After all, "it takes a village to raise a child " – unknown

Private
Only members can see who's in the group and what they post.

Members · 40

Johanna is an admin.

_____

Activity

One new post today

Posts

Johanna Schafer
15m

Just wanted to say that it was so nice seeing everyone at the potluck this past weekend. It should be an annual end-of-summer event! I think every single house in the neighborhood was represented!

👍 💜 Maria Fuchs, Eva Keller and 26 others
13 comments   1 share

View more comments

Eva Keller

It was lovely, thank you for hosting, Johanna! Though, I don't think EVERY house was represented... the "For Sale" sign went down on the Schulz's old house Tuesday morning. Has anyone met the folks who bought it? I haven't seen a single moving truck there any of the last three days.

Hannah Zimmermann

I've seen a car go in and out a few times. It looks like it's a young woman, and I think she has a baby? I saw a stroller in the driveway, but that's about it. I was thinking of going over this weekend to introduce myself.

Maria Fuchs

I'd be happy to go with you, Hannah. I wonder if she's the woman Kaiser has seen the last few nights coming home from work. She's been pushing a stroller up and down the street around midnight. He thought it was a little strange, but I figured the baby is colicky or something, and she's trying to get him to sleep.

Johanna Schafer

Oh my gosh, I'm so glad you said that. That makes so much sense now... I was terrified the other night!

Maria Fuchs

@JohannaShafer, what do you mean?

Johanna Schafer

Just that, I couldn't sleep myself, so I got up to get my e-reader out of my office. The window was open, and I heard a woman's voice singing the creepiest lullaby! I thought I was hearing someone's television out of *their* open window, but if the new neighbor has a baby that's fussy and she's been pushing him in the stroller at night, that makes me feel so much better!

Hannah Zimmermann
What was the lullaby?

Johanna Schafer
It was nothing I'd ever heard before. And it was in English. Something about taking what she needed to fill her darling's belly beneath the moon. She's probably just at her wit's end with a colicky baby, making things up on two hours of sleep to keep herself from going crazy. Anyway, I'll go over to meet her too. Tomorrow?

Hannah Zimmermann
See you then!

THE BLOOD-STARVED ROMANIAN VAMPIRE WOMEN FROM SPACE

Sean Malia Thompson

He remembers being so drunk he could barely stand. Another bad night, remembering her. Aching to see her. To feel her. A trip through Europe to try to get his head straight.

All just distraction. The typical obtuse American, backpacking. He felt worse than ever. He missed her worse than ever. A deep ache in his chest, a sort of metaphysical wound.

So, the small town an hour out of Bucharest. Walking as the sun set, seeing the Carpathian mountains painted orange and pink. And then the bar. Then alcohol. A shitload of it. That peel the paint from the wall plum shit, Tuica.

He has a vague recollection of two women. Local. Enticing. Dark hair, tight jeans, intoxicating perfumes. Toasting to nothing at all. Kissing them both. The watery look to everything, soon enough the room spinning. Cutting in and out of consciousness like a choppy film edit.

And now he has a headache fit to crack his skull in two, waking up in a pile of his own vomit. In a cold, dark room. His blue jeans frozen to his legs, his leather jacket dusted with frost. His long blonde hair, slicked back with product crinkles, like cellophane when he tries to smooth it out.

The floor is a black metal. Iron? Lead? A distant glow barely illuminates the room. He can barely see anything. Just the breath in front of his face. His neck hurts like a bitch. He touches the sore spot, hissing as his fingers make contact.

"Christ!"

There's a shape, in a chair in the corner.

"Hey, where are we?"

The figure doesn't respond, or move.

The room has elaborate sconces along the walls, currently not lit. A painting of the countryside he can barely make out. A large stone fireplace.

"God damn it," he says, closing the distance "I'm talking to—"

He touches the figure's shoulder, shaking him. The head rolls off to thump wetly to the floor.

"Shit!"

There is a flashlight in the hand of the headless corpse. He grabs the thing and pushes the button, beam cutting through the darkness. There are stairs leading up. Seeing no other option, he hustles up them.

The stairs terminate at a dark corridor that seems to stretch on for miles in either direction. An ornate castle hallway. Paintings on the walls, furniture, metal chandeliers shining in darkness.

He proceeds forward, every creak of footfall making him want to run screaming like a rabbit. The cold is enveloping him as he shivers and huddles. A bright red pentagram carpet. A painting of a headless man with his eyes torn from his head.

He wraps his black leather jacket around himself, tighter against the cold. Chanting emanates from down the hall.

He has no weapons. He's cursing himself for not

checking the last room for a pipe, a stick, anything.

There's still time, he thinks, *I could just go back.* Yet, his feet lead him forward, almost against the commands of his mind. He can feel air coming from an opening to the right, and along with this comes a sickly sweet scent, like rotting fruit. He dares a glance into the room off of the hall and feels his jaw drop.

A huge room with a tall ceiling leading off out of sight, with rounded walls of the same dark metal. Sharp scythes, and long blades mounted along the back of the room. An elaborate rug of bright reds, greens, and blues, with a concentric design in the center of gold circles and squares, appearing as a uniform and sharp design.

Tall things in black cloaks, huddled around a trash can fire, chanting in an alien language. Gargantuan, lithe creatures, graceful in their way. Seven feet tall if they are an inch; long, almost venous hands with protruding, jagged yellow claws. Furry, white snouts, reminiscent of Mustelidae—this is all that can be seen poking from the cowls. Black, vertical stripes line the muzzles like Zebra stripes. Long, blood-stained teeth. On the grate of the garbage can fire is a human leg.

"Holy shit," he whispers to himself, terrified the creatures will hear.

Never mind them, lover.

In his head. Her voice. He almost answers out loud, he is so out of it, so absolutely off kilter. He could float away at any moment. It would not surprise him in the slightest.

He travels down the hallway full of shadows and a terrible chill. More paintings. A group of three women, all in 19th century garb. Black hair done up in buns with flower pins, the fashion of the time. All in bright white dresses, shining through the oils of the canvas. They are the two women he met at the bar. And the one in the center is his love. The other painting is a field of crucified men and women, the mud below stained with blood.

A new room on his left. A huge pen of some sort, the

scent of hay on the ground, and a putrid scent, mixed with the waste of farmyard animals. The walls are of wood, mimicking a barn. Neon green, canine-like creatures with six legs and no tails, yipping and snapping at each other, heads skeletal and gaunt. Big eyes that go all the way down the face: lightning eyes, that same shocking hue. Bulbous, muscular appendages, coated in the neon green fur. They fight over a ravaged human arm.

He passes a room with an enormous stained-glass window, the design depicting a woman in a white floral dress reaching to the heavens. Skinless corpses are stacked in a pile on the floor, surrounded by lit, black candles. He passes a room full of naked men and women, all copulating in blood that spills from stone dragon head fountains at all four sides of the room; they eat human flesh off of body parts stacked on silver trays. He passes a room with a waterfall of blood, and a square metal pool, small children in bathing suits waving to him, playing on inflatable tubes. He passes a room with a heavy metal band, leather jackets and long hair thrashing. Just like a large, seedy nightclub, complete with neon light show. A pit of metalheads sets upon a handful of naked people, all screaming for help he knows he can't possibly provide.

You like all of this. I can tell. We picked you for a reason, lover. You are like us.

"I'm nothing like you."

The dark, cold hallway finally leads to a large room, opening wide, the walls expanding outward. Swords along the walls, decorative rugs of gold with dark red, arabesque designs. The women are all in lacy bras and panties, flowing, black silk scarves, dark hair down, skin pale as milk. Draped on golden chairs with crushed red velvet trim. The mixture of a medieval castle and a spaceship—the combination leaves his mind reeling. Complicated terminals of flashing lights, brightly colored control panels of neon reds, greens, blues, and purples. An enormous bronze chandelier of black candles hanging high above. Stone, spiral staircases leading to higher floors, hidden in shadow. Behind them is a huge window, leading out to nothing but the blackest blackness he has ever seen. Stars. So many stars.

One of the women from the bar floats over to him, her eyes green. She lightly caresses his face with the back of a hand with long, green fingernails.

"So nice to see you finally awake," she says, kissing his neck, before he pushes her off. She shrugs and floats off to the corner of the room.

"Yes, we can't wait to have fun with you," another woman says, floating over, black silk fluttering behind, her eyes a dark blue, her fingernails the same dark navy. This woman grabs his crotch and he can't help himself he lets out an audible gasp, before he—perhaps with slightly less conviction—pushes her aside.

Because now she is approaching: his true love. The one who abandoned him a year ago. The girl he met at the nightclub in Hartford, Connecticut. The girl he had fallen in love with, who always kept the strange hours; who was always gone from his bed in the morning. And now here she is, before him, eyes dark red, like blood without oxygen.

"You're a space vampire," he says.

She bursts into laughter, exposing long, canine fangs. Her lipstick is the same dark red as her eyes. Her scent is intoxicating, some sort of sweet, floral fragrance, yet underneath the light scent of iron, of spilt blood.

The one he loves yanks his jacket off and rips his plain black t-shirt. His heavily tattooed upper torso is exposed, and she runs her sharp, red pointer nail over his chest.

"Face it, you enjoy the pain. Look at all these upon your body. Don't tell me you did it just for the art?"

"What do you want with me? No more games. Speak plainly."

The ones with blue and green eyes grab each of his

shoulders, tight. He can't fight them off. They are far too strong.

"We are lonely. We could use some male companionship."

He leans in as much as he is able, to stare into her eyes, his face mere inches from hers.

"What, like that poor bastard you decapitated back there? Or the other people being slaughtered here?"

One behind him laughs in his ear, and the heat from her breath stirs his loins, but he forces himself to pay attention.

Keep your eyes open, he thinks, *find a way to escape.*

"Escape? Poor man, oh you *poor, deluded* man. We are in the great beyond!"

And she twirls in a circle, floating off of the ground, her black silk scarves swirling in the air about her. Her laugh is uproarious, and shakes the very room, vibrating his bones.

"We drift in a vast, black infinity. You can no more escape than you could survive!"

One of them is sucking on his neck, now. His body and mind are in a state of frenzy. He stares out at the dark void before her; the great, immense, cold vacuum. She's right. There is no escape. Even if he were to defeat them, he'd be trapped on a ship in space, with no idea how to pilot it, let alone any idea what he would do for food. He thinks back to the human leg on the grate of the trash can fire, and shudders.

Slowly, the vampire with the dark red eyes lowers to the ground before him.

"Why fight? You want us, no?"

They can read his mind, so he does not deny it. Truly, the act would be fruitless, useless. He wants them more than he has ever wanted anything. His blood itches for them. For all of them. He feels like a man who has been trapped in a blizzard, finally finding the warmth of a blazing hearth. He longs for this blessed heat-embrace, as he yearns for their skin, their bodies; to kiss them, to hold them, to find oblivion within their arms, and at the sharpness of their mouths. He will accept damnation for a single delirious day in their embrace.

"And what do I get in return?"

They are taking off his pants. His vampire love gives him an exaggerated stage pout.

"You feign ignorance, but I can see by that tent in your briefs you know *exactly* what you are going to get, and in turn we will feast upon that sweetness inside your veins. And then we shall give you the choice we rarely grant others."

She leans in, red lips pulling back to expose her fangs.

"To make death your bitch."

Her head darts forward, fast as a snake. Teeth pierce his neck and he cries out, because suddenly as he is pierced so too does he pierce her. Her red eyes roll back within her head as she moans in pleasure.

He fights for control as pain mixes with ecstasy. She is floating, legs splayed to either side of him. He can smell her, the blood and the sex of her, a maddening bouquet. The air is redolent of exsanguination and the perfumes of lust.

The others joining, sinking teeth into his pectoral muscle, into his shoulder. Black silk fluttering. They set upon him like a pack of wolves, and he is prey that, far from terrified, longs for them to rip him apart. The sensations are unlike any he has ever felt, feeling his life fade in slow degrees, as he ravages, and they in turn feast.

Staring out at the darkness, at the innumerable shining stars, rising to his peak and then finishing with such force he is shocked when he doesn't just die.

In his ear then, her words: "Make your choice." He looks into her eyes. *To be as we are, or to slip away.*

Why am I even trying to escape? he wonders to himself. *Would it really be so terrible to live forever on a spaceship with beautiful, undead women?*

"Make me as you are."

She stops sucking the blood from his neck, and slices open the top of her right breast, bringing his mouth in. He drinks deeply of her blood, feeling like he's swallowing down ounce after ounce of scalding venom. His eyes roll back into his head, and he feels the mixture of bliss and horror. His life slips away, to be replaced by a different form of existence.

Weeks go by, spent feeding on the humans they have locked in the bottom of the ship, in the dungeons. Skeletons are chained next to emaciated men and women along the stone walls. He explores the wonders and terrors the ship has to offer. A stream in a mock forest with real pines and oaks, dirt on the ground. In this fake wilderness, men and women are nailed upside down through the feet and hands to the trees. Another room with a pit of mud, in the center of which two vampire women wrestle. The winner gets a screaming man. She simply rips the head off like a berry, drinking from the neck stump. He goes in and has a drink from the head. They fuck in the mud.

A maze of colored mirrors. He gets lost for many hours. Finally, he finds a pile of bones, with a red door leading back to the hallway. He finds the same metal band again, this time playing at the top of a skateboard ramp, while gaunt looking men and women grind along the coping and flip their boards to perform tricks. He isn't terribly shocked to see a cooler full of human hearts. The skaters taking a break slam metal straws into the organs, like bloody, muscular juice boxes.

He makes love so many times to the vampire women he loses count. Different women, or the same ones, across the many chambers of the vessel. His prevailing sentiment is one of awe at the sheer immensity of the ship. New rooms and spaces reveal themselves to him. He has no idea just how large it truly is.

Yet, always he loves her. The one he belongs to. The one who turned him.

He has no idea how many weeks or months go by. With time, he is surprised to find any apprehension with killing the innocent disappears. He has absolutely no idea how to feel about this. He is changing into a thing beyond morality. He is a beast, and they are simply prey. Prey that prays, all for naught.

One night his love asks him where they should land the ship. He smiles and tells her. And she and the women with the blue and green eyes all laugh, maniacally, like absolute lunatics. Horny and hungry, beyond space and time.

The medieval castle-ship lands in the middle of the darkened street, in Bucharest. Cars smash into each other, some mount the curbs, hitting pedestrians, who fly like bloody bags. The portcullis slams to the road, sending explosions of paved road soaring through the air, as screams fill the night. He flies from the ship with his wife, Lulia, she of the red eyes and vicious nature. The green and blue-eyed vampiresses burst forth from behind them, as do the six-legged, neon green dog creatures, the tall things in the robes, and a plethora of naked vampire men and women. Running from the castle-ship, battle cries filling the air.

He and his bride lift a young man into the air, each taking one side of his neck to drain him, then tossing his body, flailing, into a building, where it smashes with a squelch. A green dog-thing gets a hold of a six year old child, its muzzle going deep into the abdomen of the boy, ripping his guts out in one long strand as the child cries for its mother. A tall creature in a robe swings a scythe that slices through an old woman's neck, sending the head flying. The creature swiftly grabs the severed head and rips a hunk from the cheek, as the eyes still blink.

The vampiresses rip and tear through a crowd of howling people trying to flee. Ripping off arms, ripping off legs. They get to either side and grab a screaming woman and rip her in half, swooping in flight to catch the blood as it is expelled into the air. The metal band rolls a wooden platform on wheels down the portcullis and hops aboard this makeshift stage, rocking out as wanton carnage is committed, Romanian humans are exsanguinated, and alien monsters devour and destroy.

"I love you, Lulia," he says, his mouth covered in blood, his eyes now red.

"And I you," the red-eyed vampire woman says, smiling wide, flashing crimson-stained fangs.

The streets are filled with blood, organs, and bodies. By day's end the vampires have taken their feed-slaves, their human blood-cattle, and turned hundreds. This new army enters the castle-ship, which launches into the sky with no discernible means of locomotion, no rocket power or even any lights below to give any hint as to how the ship flies.

The castle-ship lands somewhere within the mysterious and ancient shadows of the Carpathian Mountains. And there it sits, even now, waiting. A fortress of atrocities, a palace of nightmares. A superstructure of damnation.

LA BELLE MALADIE

Tiffany Morris

A suffering Christ glowered at them from the crucifix. Sabine led the tourists through Saint Sébastien church, inviting them to sit on the ornately carved wooden pews. They inhaled deeply, drinking in the smell of incense and dust and the vanilla-papered scent of old parchment coming from the antique Bibles and hymn books placed in each seat. In the tall windows the eponymous saint was beautiful in his own stained-glass renderings, the reds and blues surrounding his robed body casting bright light from their dalliance with the afternoon sun.

Among the visitors was a woman whose white-blonde hair shone with the same colors streaming prismatic from the window. Sabine tried not to be distracted by the woman's strikingly dark eyes, her skin that glowed in the beams of sunlight. The traveler was Odette Swain, a PhD student from Montreal whose dissertation focused on occult symbolism in the cinematic oeuvre of Edith Vallée. Sabine's bosses had been very clear that she was to meet with the scholar and talk about the possibilities of research grants, a documentary film, and other potential partnerships between the County Board of Arts and Culture and the Canadian university. Sabine had tried not to feel jealous while reading about the woman's credentials, wishing that she'd managed to stay the course in her own academic work on Vallée and the dark feminine, in the time before anxiety and self-doubt had bludgeoned her and forced her to finally drop out of graduate school altogether.

As the crowd dispersed, Sabine handed the tourists the pamphlets. They were likely in town for the festival, but it didn't hurt to remind them to be excited about the following evening's events—so much planning had gone into it this year. In addition to being the 75th anniversary of the festival, the occasion was made momentous by the discovery of Vallée's infamous lost film the previous winter. Sabine took a quick glimpse inside the pamphlet, admiring her own copy on the glossy paper.

Edith Vallée Festival du Film

The village of Petit-Etang welcomes all visitors to our celebration of the 75th year of the Edith Vallée Short Film Festival. This year's program features special screenings by directors from countries across the world, including Australia, Papua New Guinea, and Canada.

Edith Vallée was a celebrated surrealist and groundbreaking female filmmaker. Vallée was a contemporary of Jean Cocteau working in a style that combined the set styling of Georges Méliès with the mystical aesthetics of Victorian Arthuriana. Her cinematic oeuvre created a world of fairy tale menace where witches reigned supreme.

Each summer, her large historical home would fill with her coterie of creatives, becoming a one-woman economy unto herself. Petit-Etang was proud to welcome her on her annual retreats to our humble village. Her estate has graciously continued the director's financial and artistic legacy every year following the artist's death in 1948.

The Edith Vallée Festival du Film takes place on the grounds of her manor. Please join us in celebrating this pioneer of cinema with a special screening of the newly uncovered film La Belle Maladie. *Its existence was only a rumor until the footage was uncovered in an unmarked box on her property. The Board of Arts and Culture is thrilled with the discovery—no one could have known that routine restoration work would uncover such treasures lurking beneath the floorboards. La Belle Maladie will close the festival in the historic Saint Sébastien church. Please also check our local vendors' tables and enjoy immersive theatrical vignettes between screenings. Schedule of events is shown on the following pages.*

Odette hung back from the crowd, staring up at the church's vaulted ceiling. Sabine swiveled her head to mirror her gaze and admired the motes of dust that danced golden in the thick summer air. She then approached Odette. She shyly greeted her in English, relieved when the woman responded in French.

"We're so pleased to have you here," Sabine said, feeling self-conscious in the scholar's gaze.

"Thank you," Odette replied, her voice honeyed, accented by the lilting Quebec French. "I'm quite excited to visit the estate and to see *La Belle Maladie.*"

Sabine tried not to linger on the woman's face, flustered. The woman's eyes felt like they penetrated some deeper part of her. As a blush crawled over her skin, a vaguely drunken feeling washed over her, a warm ocean wave. She quickly averted her gaze.

"I've been instructed to invite you to dinner this evening," Sabine said, focusing on a spot somewhere above Odette's head. "The Board would love to host you."

"That will be fine," Odette said, still staring at her. "I'm staying at the Inn on Rue Canal."

"The restaurant is just down the street. I'll come for you at 6:30 and we can walk down."

They chatted a bit more before Sabine left the church. As she stood on the stairs, she breathed deeply of the fresh floral air, enjoying the hot sun warming her pale skin. She glimpsed the Vallée manor a few doors down the road, its windows darkened, their glaring gargoyle gaze focused down into the idyllic village. Sabine tried to ignore the foreboding that announced itself deep inside her stomach. Surely it was just nerves, stress from all the festival planning finally coming to fruition, maybe even a twinge of excitement at meeting this stranger, to talk about Vallée and the wondrous ways the director had made the fantastic feel vital, alive. Jealousy had calved itself into something else: desire, hunger, or something deeper still, left unnamed.

Three knights descended from the stage onto the grounds, their hoisted swords gleaming in the simulated firelight. Ribbons of blood stained the ornately painted armor as the gurgle of death caught in theatrical groans from each actors' throat. Children in skeleton suits with painted grinning skull faces danced among the fallen, singing in a shrill chorus. The notes formed a somber song that Sabine didn't recognize, but the impish gloom was enough to infer that it was some sort of memento mori.

The festival was moving ahead at a clip. Sabine had watched the attendees arrive, watched their awestruck faces contend with the size of the property, listened to their thrilled exclamations over the ornate marble floors of the manor's foyer. Guests were always enchanted by the experimental black and white portraits of Vallée in elaborate costumes, her face blurring realities in strange double exposures, her daguerreotype haunting gaze staring into the passerby as they made their way into the large screening room. Sabine, herself, had spent many days staring at the photos and film stills, waiting for Vallée to somehow reveal her secrets. Images from the set of *Le Rêve des Squelettes* showed strange symbols painted on naked flesh; stills from *Elle a Enterré Ses Dents* were painted over with crude drawings of human bodies, and in all of them Sabine felt something beckon to her.

Darkness engulfed the screening room as the next film began. Sabine yawned and checked her phone: 4:26 pm. She'd have to leave soon to get ready for the screening this evening. She stood and slung her purse over her shoulder, ducking out of the manor before she could be asked to help with anything else, keeping her head down to avoid eye contact with the director, a local actor whose debut she knew was some veiled therapy work about his recent breakup.

The air outside was humid, rose-scented. Invasive bushes lined the estate grounds, white petals careening their pale threat into a downy layer on the grass. The invading presence was so beautiful that she privately lamented that they'd be uprooted following the festival's conclusion. One of life's tragedies: nothing, not even something beautiful, could be eternal.

Sabine sat in the back pews, nervous excitement coursing a restless river through her body. She hadn't seen the uncovered film yet—the quality assurance had been conducted by the senior directors. As she tried to imagine the film, Odette entered the church. The scholar moved languidly through the crowd with eerie grace, each person's head either turned to her or pointedly ignoring the ethereal creature. Sabine tried desperately to be part of the latter group, though something in her couldn't resist gazing at Odette. The dinner had gone so well—the board charming, Odette engaged and compelling, the cooperative air dwindling into a playful intimacy as more people left and the night waxed on, until it was just Odette and Sabine sharing a final bottle of wine.

The kiss that she had shared with the woman in deep black night had embarrassed her too much to want to acknowledge her arrival. With a wince, Sabine recalled how Odette had insisted they go for a walk, how their bodies moved closer until finally Sabine moved in for a kiss just a few blocks from her own apartment. Wishful thinking, maybe, that they'd end up there, all of it so uncharacteristic of Sabine, who only ever longed to be so bold.

She had conjured a formerly-dormant desire in Sabine from the moment they'd first met. Odette's mouth had been yielding in the moment, but her hands had firmly touched Sabine's waist in a plea and a push all at once. She backed away from Odette quickly and they'd kept walking along the stone walls in stilted conversation that faded into slow and awkward silence. Sabine's face and neck reddened in hot, humiliated frustration for the rest of the walk until she mumbled a sullen bonne nuit and rushed inside her silent apartment building, not bothering to look back at the beautiful traveler, leaving her to find her own way back to the hotel. She hoped Odette hadn't said anything to Jacqueline, the festival director.

Odette didn't seem to notice her and took a spot near the front. Sabine stared at the back of her head, the waterfall of sleek hair that captured and refracted so much light. She couldn't hear the woman's voice as she turned to speak to Jacqueline, the two leaning close together and laughing. Dread sank a witches' stone in her stomach. All words swam to the back of the room in unknown syllables as Sabine focused only on Odette, each distant movement of her body a rhythm that her own body responded to with the cold rush of longing.

She didn't even notice when the historic film first flickered to life, a Lazarus miracle. As *La Belle Maladie* began, the screen filled with Edith Vallée's face, smiling wider and wider until her face contorted into a strange assembly of shapes vaguely representing a human. The shaking of her shoulders indicated laughter, but her mouth was unmoving. As the camera panned out, her limbs twisted into odd angles. Her body became a rictus ritual. It moved and stopped in time to the soundtrack, a combination of dreary dissonant organ notes and chanting, humming voices. A group of naked women rushed to her. One of them pulled out a sickle and slashed Vallée's stomach, her organs pulled out from her torn flesh, wet shimmering meat held joyfully in the women's bloodied hands.

Sabine stared, transfixed by the macabre spectacle. Odette was now standing, in a long white gauzy dress, dancing in front of the projection screen. The background dancers trailed out behind her, shrieking as their long gauze wings hovered in the air with every movement of their flailing arms. Odette's face was beautiful in the neon light that would be sallow as memory on anyone else. The flashing hot pink traveled over her as a burning phoenix plumage, making her perfectly tanned skin look lit from within.

Audience members screeched in unison and then stopped. Sabine's own mouth began to stretch into an involuntary grin. Vallée's face snarled and then smiled into the camera in close-up, thick black tears running down her face in bloodied rivulets. The women on the screen held her organs and meat aloft as they stood in a circle, chanting. A man in skull makeup appeared and slashed at the sky with a scythe. The film was ritual—but of and for what, Sabine couldn't possibly know—and painted-on color flashed on the film, the scene the red of meat and the green of rot, pink of the beautiful veins on Odette's eyes, Odette's dark eyes—

People dressed in robes appeared on the screen and in the aisles. Sabine held a hand to her face and realized with horror she was still grinning, could not stop grinning, as she tore with her fingernails at the corners of her mouth until something grabbed her wrist and lifted her from her seat. Several pairs of strong arms stole her into the dark basement of the church and then dragged her slow, stupid legs, moving dreamlike into an even darker corridor, deeper under the church's now-unhallowed ground.

The catacomb grinned at her through the rows of ancient skulls that lined the walls. The dull light from the candles burning on tall brass stands every few feet made the disembodied heads swim and dance to the tune of an unheard song. As she shuffled down the winding corridor, she heard it as a silent dirge celebrating what was sure to be her doom.

As they entered a sanctum with rows of stone seats, a

skeletal torso was seated at the back of the room, headless, with bright red roses woven throughout the branches of its ribs. The smell of blood traveled through the air, thick with incense and hazy with layers of heavy floral musk. Abattoir and flower shop all at once; camellias wept in long strands, twisted and gnarled into garlands with other unknown flowers, deep blushing pinks and purples, genital and bright in their petaled protrusions. They surrounded an altar at the front of the room. Hooded figures sat in silence, heads bowed as penitent as parishioners seeking atonement, a wet drip thudding in dull repetition somewhere in the distance.

Sabine blinked, eyes straining as they adjusted to the sudden brightness of the room. Candles pumped yellow waxen light into the space. Their pallid fire shone over a large circle of silver containers set before the altar. Between them a massive symbol was drawn in curlicued blood on the dirty stone floor.

As she was pushed forward by a firm hand on her back the smell of blood and flowers became the smell of rotten vegetables and other, more animal, necrotic things. Her stomach heaved; revulsion, exhaustion, and terror rose up a maelstrom in her body. Legs weak, her knees trembled as every instinct urged her to free herself from their grasp and run. The robed figure behind her grabbed her arm. Perhaps the animal smell of her sweat, radiating fear, gave her away. She struggled against him but was powerless to do much before he yanked her forward—so hard she worried if it would dislocate her shoulder—and shoved her into the circle. She shrieked and fell with a dull thud onto the hard stone. Pain cracked lightning through her knees and into her back. Agony traveled through her shoulders as another shrill yell punched its way, full-throated, up from the very bottom of her gut.

Sabine pushed herself up off the ground, the cool smooth texture of the stone on her bare palm a strange relief even amid such terror. She wobbled, standing like a newborn foal on uncertain grass, and tried to steady herself. Another shriek merged with a sob as she hurtled herself out of the circle, knocking over one of the containers that oozed out a slow wave of black tar. The smell of strange, resinous flowers rose like smoke. As her pained legs burned with weakness and desperation, another robed figure grabbed her and threw her back down to the center of the bloody circle.

The others moved out from the chairs, closing in. Sabine still couldn't see their faces.

"Let me through," she screamed. "Please."

"They won't be doing that." Odette's voice, the familiar but strangely accented French, rang out, reverberating off the stone that entombed them all.

The crowd parted to let her through. Odette walked into the circle, now naked, her body shimmering with a rose-scented oil. Sabine was helpless, once more, to move under the woman's gaze.

Odette grabbed her hand and kissed it, then caressed her face before pulling in closer to her. Their mouths moved together in hot, excited rhythms as she held Sabine to the center of the circle. As the lovers took off their clothes, the crowd around them melted away into dream and nothingness, light and murmur traveling over Sabine's body as Odette's fingers entered her.

Sabine's orgasm turned her whole awareness into a hot bloom. As she opened her eyes to look at Odette, the woman's face smudged and distorted briefly into the face of Edith Vallée, moaning and smiling and staring with the same dark eyes. Sabine screamed and tried to push the woman off of her as sharp metal plunged into her chest. Odette's traitorous hand brought the gleaming ritual knife into her heart.

Blood pumped out in dark streams as Odette's wavering visage sloughed off skin and became skull. The pain was a bright, searing light tearing through and traveling out of Sabine, a river coursing into the woman on top of her. That skull slowly resumed flesh and became Edith Vallée's own, fully, as her essence adopted this new body.

She stared down at the hapless, faceless shell she had once been. An essence of her old consciousness absorbed into this new energy stream as her former body became a mere skeleton, with a grinning catacomb skull atop its limp frame. The flame of her being grafted itself onto a new soul as memories of death filled her. She screamed what remained of Sabine into nothingness.

Edith grinned wide, feeling the muscles of her new body. The bones beneath her were beautiful in the candlelight, its hands grasping at her flesh that was now, finally, made eternal.

ABOUT THE AUTEURS

Brian O'Connell is currently in the process of completing his B.A. in Film Analysis and Criticism at Hunter College. Some other essays of his on the horror genre have been published online at *The Plutonian*. His favorite Euroschlock movies, at the time of this writing, are *Phenomena* (Argento, 1985) and *The Iron Rose* (Rollin, 1973). You can find him on Twitter at @_Sheehogue_.

Patrick Lacey was born and raised in a haunted house. He spends his time writing novels like *Bad Movie Night, Where Stars Won't Shine,* and *A Voice So Soft*. He lives in a hopefully un-haunted house in Massachusetts with two hyperactive cats, his daughter, and his wife. Follow him on Twitter (@patlacey).

Matthew M. Bartlett's self-published debut *Gateways to Abomination* signaled the arrival of a distinctive new voice in horror. He is the author of several short story collections including *Creeping Waves* and *Where Night Cowers*, and a new novel entitled *The Obsecration*. He has recorded several spoken word records and has stories published in a variety of anthologies and journals. In late 2020 he joined the Great Resignation, immediately launching his current ongoing project, now in its third year: a subscription service for monthly illustrated chapbooks, entitled *The WXXT Program Guide*. He lives in Western Massachusetts with his wife Katie Saulnier (whose art graces the cover of *Gateways to Abomination*) and their cats Peachpie and Larry.

doungjai gam is the author of *glass slipper dreams, shattered* and *watch the whole goddamned thing burn*. Her short fiction and poetry have been published in *LampLight*, *Wicked Haunted*, *Cape Cod Poetry Review*, and *Unquiet Sisters: Essays by Asian Women in Horror*, among other places. Born in Thailand, she currently resides in southern Connecticut with author Ed Kurtz and their cats Daria and Lucia.

Mer Whinery is a storyteller of the rural macabre from southeastern Oklahoma. He enjoys sunny autumn afternoons and wandering about in forlorn burial grounds, dressed all in black with a thoughtful look upon his face. He loves horror video games but covers his ears if they get too loud and relies on his oldest child to get him past the jump-out parts. He is the author of *The Country Girl's Guide to Hexes and Haints*, *The Little Dixie Horror Show* and *Trade Yer Coffin for a Gun*. He resides somewhere in Oklahoma with his wife Annie and his two sons Kameron and Harper.

Gwendolyn Kiste is the three-time Bram Stoker Award-winning author of *The Rust Maidens*, *Reluctant Immortals*, *Boneset & Feathers*, *Pretty Marys All in a Row*, and *The Haunting of Velkwood*. Her short fiction and nonfiction have appeared in outlets including *Lit Hub*, *Nightmare*, *Best American Science Fiction and Fantasy*, *Vastarien*, Tor Nightfire, Titan Books, and *The Dark*. She's a Lambda Literary Award winner, and her fiction has also received the This Is Horror award for Novel of the Year as well as nominations for the Premios Kelvin, Ignotus, and Dragon Awards. Originally from Ohio, she now resides on an abandoned horse farm outside of Pittsburgh with her husband, their excitable calico cat, and not nearly enough ghosts. Find her online at gwendolynkiste.com

Sam Richard is the author of *Grief Rituals*, *Sabbath of the Fox-Devils*, and the Wonderland Award-Winning Collection *To Wallow in Ash & Other Sorrows*. He is the editor of several anthologies, including the Splatterpunk Award-Nominated *The New Flesh: A Literary Tribute to David Cronenberg*, *Stories of the Eye,* and *Cinema Viscera*. His short fiction litters the landscape of various anthologies and magazines. Widowed in 2017, he slowly rots in Minneapolis where he runs Weirdpunk Books. You can stalk him @SammyTotep on socials or www.weirdpunkbooks.com.

Thomas Breen's stories have been published in numerous anthologies and periodicals, and he is the author of two books about American religion. A former journalist, he lives and works in North Central Connecticut. His story in this anthology was inspired by a bus trip from Dublin to Glendalough, which, despite the events depicted in the story, he wholeheartedly recommends.

Orrin Grey is a skeleton who likes monsters and the author of several spooky books, including *How to See Ghosts & Other Figments*. Besides scary stories, he writes tabletop roleplaying games, essays about horror films, and anything else that people will pay for. You can visit him in the beyond at orringrey.com.

Christa Carmen is the Bram Stoker Award-nominated author of *The Daughters of Block Island* (Thomas & Mercer) and *Something Borrowed, Something Blood-Soaked* (Unnerving). Additional work can be found in *Vastarien*, *Nightmare*, *Orphans of Bliss*, *Year's Best Hardcore Horror*, and the Stoker-nominated anthologies, *Not All Monsters* and *The Streaming of Hill House*. She has a BA from the University of Pennsylvania, an MA from Boston College, and an MFA from the University of Southern Maine. Christa lives in Rhode Island with her husband, daughter, and bloodhound-golden retriever mix.

Sean Malia Thompson lives in Santa Fe with his long-time partner. He grew up in central Massachusetts, surrounded by trees, and not much else. He has a Bachelor's degree in English from The University of Massachusetts, in Dartmouth. He is owner and editor of Nictitating Books, and has edited and published the Shirley Jackson and Elgin award-winning releases *We Are Here to Hurt Each Other* by Paula D. Ashe and *Elegies of Rotting Stars* by Tiffany Morris. He is the author of the mosaic novel *They Never Find the Bodies in Whispering Pines*, the possession novel *TH3 D3MON*, and the absurdist slasher novels *God Damn Zombie Chainsaw Murderer*, and *Another God Damn Zombie Chainsaw Murderer... Again*, as well as the story collections *Screaming Creatures* and *Fist of Serrated Teeth: Murder Stories*. He has been featured in such publications as *Vastarien*, *Hymns of Abomination*, *Nox Pareidolia*, *Behold the Undead of Dracula*, *Terror in 16-bits*, and *Test Patterns*, and has been featured on the *Tor Nightfire* site and in *Rue Morgue* magazine.

Tiffany Morris is an L'nu'skw (Mi'kmaw) writer from Nova Scotia. She is the author of the swampcore horror novella *Green Fuse Burning* (Stelliform Books, 2023) and the Elgin Award-winning horror poetry collection *Elegies of Rotting Stars* (Nictitating Books, 2022). Her work has appeared in the Indigenous horror anthology *Never Whistle At Night* (Vintage Books), as well as in *Nightmare Magazine*, *Uncanny Magazine*, and *Apex Magazine*, among others.

Trevor Henderson is a writer, illustrator and creature concept artist. His love of monsters, cryptids, ghosts, and other horrible entities is enduring and vast. When he is not drawing or writing horrible things, he is thinking about the unknowable and hostile forces working against all of humanity, and playing with his cat, who is named Boo. He lives in Toronto.

Jonathan Raab is the author of *Project Vampire Killer*, *The Haunting of Camp Winter Falcon*, and more. He edited the anthologies *Behold the Undead of Dracula: Lurid Tales of Cinematic Gothic Horror* and *Terror in 16-bits*. His short fiction has appeared in numerous magazines and anthologies, including *The Best Horror of the Year*, Volume Fourteen. He lives in Gothic upstate New York with his wife and son.

Coming Soon From Muzzleland Press

Vampyrvania the Tabletop Roleplaying Game

The Mausoleum of Gore
A Halloween TV Special

New Editions of:

Camp Ghoul Mountain Part VI: The Official
Novelization

The Secret Goatman Spookshow and Other
Psychological Warfare Operations